CW00487289

Whodunits for Smart People

10 Original Mysteries to Test Your Wits

Volume One

James A. Kennedy

Table of Contents

Murder at Blythe Manor   11

The Cold Case   43

The Perfect Alibi   73

Death at Dartford House   91

History Repeats Itself   119

The Purloined Papers   147

The Murdered Recluse   169

Midnight Sacrifice   193

The Escape Room   212

The Blind Witness   244

Author's Note

Hello, smart person! A few things to know before you dive in.

1. All of the following mysteries are solvable with a little brainpower. You'll find issues with alibis, suspects knowing things that they shouldn't, timelines that don't add up, and more. I promise not to end any story with "Oh, it turns out this barely-mentioned side character did it because he was crazy all along!"

2. Unlike my books of riddles and brainteasers, these whodunits are designed to be completed by one person, not together in a group setting. You probably won't want to read these mysteries out loud to friends or family, as some of them are quite long. I can't be held legally responsible for sore throats.

3. If you're stuck after reaching the turning point of the case, each story includes three hints. Each clue is slightly more

helpful than the last. Don't be too proud to use them! These whodunits are quite challenging, even for a top-notch intellect like yours.

4. These stories are written for adults, but there isn't any profanity or explicit content. However, there's plenty of murder, kidnapping, violence, infidelity, and other bad behavior. Parents, use your discretion.

Now, let's crack some cases, shall we?

Meet the Inspector

Inspector Annabel Green has worked in British law enforcement for the past 25 years. She is shrewd, impatient, and pragmatic, with a sharp eye for inconsistencies. Over the course of her career, she has gained a reputation for solving England's most challenging cases.

Although her intellectual powers are formidable, Inspector Green wouldn't stand out in a crowd: average height, average weight, pale skin, brown eyes, and shoulder-length light brown hair. The inspector uses her nondescript appearance to her advantage, and she is often underestimated by the criminals she investigates.

The product of an English father and an American mother, Annabel grew up outside London but spent many childhood summers in the southern United States. As a result, she unconsciously slips back and forth between British and American slang, much to the amusement of her friends and colleagues.

Six months ago, Inspector Green moved from central London to the small county of Dartshire, England, to be closer to her aging father. Although she tries to convince herself that she enjoys the slow pace of life and the simplicity of small-town living, she misses the excitement and drama of working in a big city.

Luckily for the inspector, an unprecedented crime wave is about to hit sleepy, peaceful Dartshire. You'll be joining Inspector Green on 10 of her toughest cases. Can you solve the mystery before she does?

Dartshire County Map

1. Ashworth
2. Chessingfield
3. Rosingham
4. Mansford
5. Sterwood Chase

6. Effington
7. Petersborne
8. Pembley
9. Norchester
10. Hazelford

Case #1:
Murder at Blythe Manor

Ashworth - May

Inspector Annabel Green sat at her desk, chin in hand, and watched a thick curtain of rain pour down outside. She hated to admit it, but she was bored. Since moving to Dartshire, she spent most of her time resolving petty disputes between neighbors. Last week's most dramatic incident: a flock of sheep grazing in the wrong field. Not exactly high-octane adventure.

Her mobile rang. A case, perhaps! Her spirits lifted and she answered immediately. "Inspector Green speaking."

"Are you interested in renewing your car's auto warranty?" asked a cheerful, robotic voice. "You might be eligible for–"

Green groaned and hung up, irritation mounting. She contemplated eating lunch, just for something to do, but it was only 10:00 in the morning. Maybe she should go commit a crime, just so she could solve it?

This train of thought was mercifully interrupted as the front door banged open. Superintendent Reginald Young strode into the police station, water dripping off his bald head. He barked, "Green! My office, now."

When Annabel was a rookie, she lived in terror of senior officers like Superintendent Young. Even when delivering praise, the man sounded impatient and irritated. She had gotten used to his gruff demeanor over the past six months and no longer panicked when summoned to his office.

By the time she walked in, the superintendent had hung up his raincoat and seated himself behind his computer. After a few seconds of furious staccato typing, he looked up and gave her what passed for a smile. The inspector knew that deep, deep down, he liked her.

"Back in London, you specialized in complex, high-profile cases," growled Young. "We've got one with your name written all over it. Blythe Manor, in Ashworth. The family's live-in butler has been murdered. I'd like you to take the lead on this one."

Inspector Green hid her excitement and responded with a blank face, "Of course, sir."

"It should take you about 30 minutes to drive down there. Take Jones with you," continued the superintendent. "I don't need to tell you that murder is extremely rare in these parts, so keep me updated. I'd like a full report on my desk by the end of the day."

The inspector nodded and said, "Yes, sir." She turned on her heel, already feeling adrenaline coursing through her veins, and collected Sergeant Jones from his desk.

Sergeant David Jones was an affable man in his early 30s. He had curly brown hair and dimples that made him look younger than he was. He was forever trying and failing to give up smoking at the request of his long-suffering girlfriend, Fiona.

The drive down to Ashworth was miserable due to the heavy rain. They crawled along the motorway, then through winding, narrow lanes with tall hedgerows on each side.

"Murder! We never get a murder case 'round here," said Jones, with barely-suppressed excitement in his voice. "Not since I've been on the force. This is the first one in ages."

"Yes, Dartshire is a remarkably well-behaved county," replied Green, squinting at the road through the blur of the windscreen wipers. "Do you know anything about Blythe Manor?"

"A bit," said Jones. "It's your typical country estate. You know: old paintings, velvet curtains, high-ceilinged rooms that no one ever uses. When I was growing up, it was a private house, but now it's open to the public on weekends. Fiona took her mum there last month, actually. Watch for that tractor."

Mentally cursing Britain's narrow roads, the inspector edged the car left into a hawthorn hedge to let a large tractor pass by.

"People say the traffic is bad in London, but at least there I never risked getting flattened by a combine harvester," muttered the inspector.

"Cheer up, old girl!" said the sergeant brightly. "We've got a murder waiting for us!"

***

At last, they reached Blythe Manor. Even with the rain obscuring the view, it was an impressive structure. Built in 1730, the three-story building was a model of Georgian architecture: immaculate red brick, dozens of white-trimmed windows, and perfect symmetry.

Surveying the extensive grounds, Inspector Green spotted a small brick cottage toward the left edge of the property.

Green and Jones hurried from the car to the front door, where a uniformed officer let them inside. Shrugging off their raincoats, they found themselves in a large foyer facing a wide wooden staircase. Several paintings of the British countryside hung on the walls. As Jones had predicted, the house looked as if it hadn't been redecorated since the late 18th century.

A well-dressed, middle-aged man walked through the doorway on the left. He turned, and called to someone out of sight, "Charlie, the detectives have arrived." He then turned back to the officers and held out his hand.

"I'm Matthew Blythe. Thank you for coming, and I hope that you can resolve this situation quickly and discreetly," he said. He was a short man with thick brown hair and close-set eyes. "William Cranston was a loyal member of our staff and we will miss him greatly."

A slender middle-aged woman emerged from the left door and joined her husband. She had shoulder-length red hair and a dusting of freckles on her cheeks. She said softly, "Charlotte Blythe. A pleasure to meet you."

Matthew said, gesturing behind him, "The study is down this hallway, to the right. That's where the murder took place. We suspect it was a botched robbery, as the room is in shambles. Luckily, nothing was taken, as far as we know."

He continued, "Obviously, you have complete access to the house and surrounding grounds. Please let us know what we can do to help the investigation."

"Lord and Lady Blythe, rest assured that you are in good hands," said Inspector Green. "We'll start by looking around the study, then move onto interviews. Please don't leave the property, as we'll need to speak to you both in the next hour."

Matthew Blythe nodded stiffly and said, "We will stay in the drawing room until summoned. Come, Charlie." Putting his hand on his wife's lower back, he herded her back into the room on the left.

"First impressions, Jones?" asked Green quietly as they walked down the hallway.

"They seem like two perfectly ordinary toffs," said Jones. "They both seem shaken by what happened, and neither strikes me as a murderer."

"I bet there's more going on under the surface," replied Green. "I look forward to speaking to each of them alone, especially the wife. I can't imagine she gets many opportunities to speak her mind."

***

Green and Jones pushed open the study door and Jones let out a low whistle. The room had been ransacked. Books had been torn off the built-in shelves and the desk had been overturned. An ornate stained-glass lamp lay broken on the floor. The large window behind the desk was wide open.

Despite the chaos, their eyes were immediately drawn to the dead body lying face-up in the middle of the room. The man had a bullet wound in the center of his forehead, and blood had pooled on the carpet underneath his wispy white hair.

Cranston was immaculately dressed in a gray suit and waistcoat, and even in death his tie remained perfectly straight. The inspector noticed that his nails were trimmed and impeccably clean.

A white-coated figure was kneeling next to the body. The inspector recognized Dr. Erin Kingsley, the DPD's chief medical examiner. Kingsley turned her head, stood up, and greeted them with a big smile. Green suspected that she was thrilled to have a real murder on her hands.

"Hi, Kingsley," said Green. "What do you have for us this morning?"

"A man, approximately 70 years old, shot in the head at close range," responded Kingsley brightly. "Only one gunshot wound, but it was enough to kill him instantly. No other cuts, abrasions, or other noticeable injuries."

"Time of death?" asked Jones.

"Sometime between 8:00 and 11:00 last night," said Kingsley. "I'll be able to tell you more once I've completed the full autopsy."

"And there's no chance it was suicide?" asked Jones.

"It's technically possible, based on the wound, but I can't imagine how. There's no gunshot residue on the hands, and the search team hasn't found a gun anywhere in the study."

Kingsley paused, then asked hopefully, "Can we remove the body now that you've seen it *in situ*? I want to get cracking... no pun intended."

"Go right ahead," said the inspector. The detectives slowly walked around the perimeter of the room as Kingsley and her assistants covered the body with a white sheet and loaded it onto a gurney. Green looked closely at the broken lamp, noting that it was still plugged into the wall.

Constable Zachary Wilkes appeared in the doorway and said, "Inspector, we recovered a handgun from the garden. We found it in the hedge about six feet left of that window." He pointed toward the large open window. The pouring rain had infiltrated the study, soaking into the thick red carpet.

Wilkes continued, "We'll run tests this afternoon to confirm that it's the murder weapon, but it looks very likely. There aren't many unaccounted-for guns in England."

"Anything unusual about the weapon?" asked Jones.

"Just your bog-standard single-action revolver," said Wilkes. "No fingerprints. It's been wiped clean. Do you want to take a look?"

"Later. I think we should start interviewing the household while their memories are still fresh," said Green. "Excellent work, Zach."

Wilkes smiled and left the room.

"Curious, that," said Inspector Green thoughtfully. "The murder weapon thrown out into the hedge. The room ransacked, but nothing missing. That stained-glass lamp alone would have fetched a good price."

"Let's talk to the Blythes–separately–and see if they can shed any light."

***

They summoned Matthew Blythe into the dining room. He sat across from them at the table, looking at ease. This was a man who was used to getting what he wanted. Even a gruesome murder in his own home couldn't faze him for long.

"Lord Blythe, tell us about your relationship with William Cranston," said the inspector.

"Blythe Manor is my family home, and I've lived here my entire life," said Matthew. "Cranston has been our butler for almost 40 years, since I was 12. He and his wife Marie live in the small caretaker's cottage on the grounds."

"How would you describe Mr. Cranston?" asked Jones.

"I'm afraid that I don't actually know him very well," said Matthew. "Both of my parents discouraged forming friendships with household staff, and even after they passed, I've never been particularly close with him. But he has been a loyal, reliable butler. I have no cause to complain."

"Do you have a security system or cameras anywhere on the property?" asked Jones.

"No, this is a very safe area and we've never had any issues with crime," said Matthew, a bit crossly. "The Cranstons are the only other people with a key to the house. I'll be looking into security systems now, of course. Charlie doesn't feel safe here anymore, poor lamb."

"Can you describe your movements last night?" asked Green.

"Of course. Charlie and I took the train to London at 5:15. We walked around Mayfair and ate dinner at Benson's," said Matthew. "We were supposed to see a show on the West End but Charlie had a cracking headache so we came home instead. We were both in bed by 10:00 last night. Charlie fell asleep immediately and I read a novel in bed for about an hour."

"Can you think of anyone who might hold a grudge against Cranston?" asked Green.

For the first time, Matthew looked slightly uncomfortable. "I've been going back and forth about telling you something. It's… a personal matter. However, I have a great respect for the British police force and I trust that you will handle this with discretion. Do I have your word that it won't be shared outside this room?"

"Lord Blythe, unless it's crucial to the prosecution, we won't repeat this information to anyone," said Jones reassuringly.

"Well," said Matthew hesitantly. "I have been engaged in a… romantic relationship with a woman in the village for the past year. Her name is Sandra Fielding. My wife does not know about this."

"I see," said Jones encouragingly. The detectives waited.

"Cranston found out about this relationship. I still don't know how, as Sandy and I have been very discreet. Regardless, he disapproved," said Matthew haltingly.

"Was he blackmailing you?" asked Sergeant Jones.

"Of course not," Matthew said. "Cranston would never stoop to blackmail. But he said if I didn't confess the truth to Charlie by her birthday, he would tell her about Sandy. Cranston has never really liked Charlie but he said she didn't deserve to be mistreated."

"And Lady Blythe's birthday is…?" asked the inspector.

"Next Tuesday," said Matthew.

"I know how it looks," he continued quickly. "But I would never have touched a hair on his head. I'm not a violent man… I was going to tell Charlie last night after the show. And this whole conversation is irrelevant! This was a robbery gone wrong!"

"Lord Blythe, we appreciate your candor," said Green. "You're absolutely sure that nothing is missing from the study?"

"After they covered the body, the police let us back into the study to look around," said Matthew. "Neither Charlie nor I spotted any missing objects, though it's quite a mess in there. We keep all of our valuables in the bank. At most, they would have gotten some first editions of rare books."

"Thank you, Lord Blythe. We'll let you know if we have additional questions," said Inspector Green. "Please return to the drawing room and ask your wife to come in next."

Matthew stood up, gave an awkward half-bow, and walked out of the dining room.

***

A minute later, Charlotte Blythe entered the room and perched delicately at the end of a chair, clutching a tissue in her hands. As the interview progressed, she slowly tore the tissue into tiny shreds.

"Lady Blythe, you are the one who found the body this morning, correct?" asked Inspector Green gently.

"Yes, I went into the study to grab a book after breakfast. He was just lying there on the floor. It… it was horrible. I've never seen a dead body before," said Charlotte with a slight quaver in her voice.

"Can you tell me about your relationship with the deceased?" asked the inspector.

"I've known William Cranston since Matthew and I started seeing each other," said Charlotte. "That would have been about… 15 years ago. My family is well-off but not to the level where you employ live-in staff. It was certainly an adjustment to get used to a butler's constant presence in my home."

"As far as my relationship with Cranston, we were never close," continued Charlotte softly. "He's always disapproved of me, for some unknown reason. I've actually been trying to convince Matthew to get rid of him for the past year or so."

"Because he dislikes you?" asked Inspector Green.

"No, I can live with that. It's the cost," said Charlotte. "This estate costs a fortune to maintain, like most of the stately homes around England. There's always repair work to be done. We're not in a desperate financial situation, but cutting full-time staff would be an easy way to reduce our expenditures."

"You might have noticed the signs on your drive over," continued Charlotte. "We've started allowing the public to visit on weekends. We've hired several part-time guides who give tours of the house and the gardens. It's been fairly successful thus far. I was planning on turning the Cranstons' cottage into a tea room for visitors, though that seems a bit cruel now. To Marie, I mean."

"Do you know anyone who disliked William Cranston?" asked Green.

"I'm not involved in his personal life at all," said Charlotte, tucking a strand of red hair behind her ear. "I haven't the faintest idea."

She continued, unprompted, "Even though I didn't really care for him, I do feel sorry for Marie. They were very close, and he's done everything for her since her arthritis worsened a few years ago. Matthew went to break the news to her this morning, and she hasn't left the cottage all day. She's in a bad state. I suppose I should go check on her after this…"

"After we're done with interviews, I'll have an officer escort you over," said the inspector. "But first, please describe your movements yesterday evening."

"We spent the evening in London," Charlotte said. "We ate an early dinner at Benson's and we were supposed to see a 7:30 showing of *The Mousetrap* but I developed a terrible headache after the meal. Matthew was nice enough to skip the show and take me home. I took a sleeping pill and was asleep by 10:00."

"What medication and dosage do you take? Would you have noticed if Lord Blythe left the bedroom?" asked Green.

"I take 10 milligrams of Zimovane, but I'm still a light sleeper," said Charlotte. "I would have definitely woken up if Matthew had gone anywhere."

"Thank you, Lady Blythe," the inspector said. "You can return to the drawing room. We'll be in touch if we have further questions."

"Oh, and you should ask your husband about a woman named Sandra Fielding," said Jones.

Charlotte looked at the sergeant quizzically and nodded before leaving the room.

"Jones…" said Green, with reproach in her voice. "I'm not sure that was very wise."

"I don't like cheaters!" said Jones defensively. "And anyways, if they're at each other's throats, the Blythes are less likely to cover for each other. That's strategy, that is."

Exasperated, Green shook her head and asked the constable to bring in Marie Cranston, the butler's wife.

***

Marie was a frail woman of about 70. Her gray hair was tucked up in a loose bun and she wore thin-rimmed silver glasses and a navy-blue long-sleeved dress. She looked dazed and lost, almost like a child.

"Mrs. Cranston, I'm so sorry for your loss," said the inspector. "We will take up very little of your time, as we know you're grieving."

Marie said slowly, "Thank you. Please ask anything you'd like." She sat down with her hands resting on her lap, and the inspector noticed that her knuckles were swollen.

"First, can you tell me about your relationship with your husband?" asked Inspector Green. "From what the Blythes have told us, you've been together for quite some time."

"William and I have been married for 45 wonderful years," said Marie. "We met while we were both working at another property. I was a housemaid; he was a footman. I knew right away that he was the love of my life. We were married within a few months."

She rummaged through her bag and produced a picture of a much-younger William, wearing his butler uniform: gray suit, white shirt, black tie, white gloves, gray waistcoat. "This is my William, just a few days after he started here."

"He looks like a fine chap. But I have to ask, did he have any enemies?" asked Jones. "Anyone who might be holding a grudge against him?"

"Not one," said Marie. "He spent almost all of his time here on this property. He would occasionally run errands or nip out for a pint with friends, but that's it. He wasn't on bad terms with anybody in the village."

"I apologize if this question offends you, but did you have a life insurance policy for your husband?" asked Sergeant Jones.

"Yes, we took out a policy three or four years ago. William said he wouldn't live forever and he wanted to make sure I was taken care of. I haven't worked in some time due to these," said Marie, holding up her gnarled hands.

"Do you have any idea of the payout you'll be receiving?" Jones followed up.

"I don't know, exactly. It's quite a lot. Around a million pounds. But I would give it all up to have my William back!" She started to cry softly.

The inspector offered Marie a tissue, which she clumsily took and dabbed at her eyes. "Where were you yesterday evening?" she asked.

"The Ashworth Amateur Dramatic Society was putting on *A Midsummer Night's Dream* at 8:00 last night," said Marie. "I'm not particularly keen on Shakespeare but my friend Jane's son had a starring role. It was held outside, in the Norbridge Park amphitheater. The show hadn't been going but 20 minutes when the heavens opened and it started pouring."

She continued, "We waited 10 minutes to see if the rain would stop, but it didn't. Jane gave me a lift back to the cottage. I got home around 9:00 p.m. and assumed William was out drinking at his usual pub, the Tipsy Ferret. I went straight to bed."

"It was only when I woke up in the morning and he still wasn't home that I started to worry. And then when Lord Blythe knocked on the cottage door… oh, that's when I knew something was wrong. Lord Blythe never visits."

She started crying in earnest. "My poor William. My poor darling. There was so much blood. And I'll never forget the look on his face."

"Thank you, Mrs. Cranston," said Inspector Green, patting her shoulder gingerly. "We appreciate your time. Please head to the drawing room and join the Blythes. We'll be with you shortly."

Wiping her eyes and sniffling, the grieving widow left the room.

***

Jones said, "Her grief seems genuine, but a million pounds is a compelling motive. Lord Blythe could have done it to save his marriage. And Lady Blythe could have done it to get rid of a man who disliked her and stood in the way of extra income."

"True… but I think I know who did it. The autopsy will confirm my suspicions," said Inspector Green, typing out a quick text message. "One of those people knew something that they shouldn't have. Once you see this, then the pieces of this unusual case fall into place."

Who knew too much?

HINTS

HINT #1:
Read again through the interviews with the household members.

HINT #2:
Which of the people in Blythe Manor had seen the dead body?

HINT #3:
Two people were involved in William Cranston's death.

ANSWER

Sergeant Jones looked at Inspector Green expectantly, waiting for more details. "Well, don't leave me in suspense," said Jones. "Who murdered him?"

"It wasn't murder," said Green. "It was suicide."

"SUICIDE?" responded Jones incredulously. "How in the world did Cranston kill himself and manage to get rid of the gun? You heard Kingsley, there's no way!"

"Marie wouldn't get a penny from the life insurance company if it was suicide, so he had to make it look like murder," said Green.

"That doesn't explain anything. Start from the beginning," said Jones, sitting back in his chair.

"This is speculation, but I'm guessing Cranston was recently diagnosed with an incurable illness," said Green. "Something where all parties involved suffer greatly and death is slow to come. The autopsy will reveal if I'm right."

"Cranston didn't want to put Marie through that. Sure, she'd eventually receive the life insurance payout after he passed, but it could take years. He would have to stop working at some point and they would struggle. How could she look after him when she needs a caretaker herself?"

"Cranston hatched a plan, and I don't think Marie knew about it. He picked a date and a time when the house would be completely empty. His wife was attending a play until 10:30 and his employers were both in London until midnight," said Green. "He couldn't have known about the unexpected rainstorm or the headache that caused them to return early and become suspects."

She continued, "Cranston wanted it to appear as if he had been killed by a robber, which is why he ransacked the study. He then took the gun—no idea where he got it, but I'm sure we'll find out—and shot himself in the head at point-blank range."

Jones said, "Okay… but why weren't his hands covered in gunshot residue? "

Green smiled. "Simple. He was wearing his usual white gloves."

"I'm sorry to say it, but you're losing your touch," said Jones. "There weren't any gloves on the scene."

"Of course there weren't," said Green. "Marie took them with her."

"Marie's in on it too?!" spluttered Jones. "Stop talking rubbish."

Green ignored him and continued, "When Marie came home early from the play, I bet she found a note in the cottage that told her what he had done and gave her a list of instructions."

"She entered the house through the door that Cranston left unlocked for her, went to the study, removed the gloves, threw the gun out of the window, locked the back door with her key, and returned to the cottage before the Blythes came home."

"What proof do you have that she was involved?" asked Jones.

"In her interview, Marie mentioned seeing his face after he died," said Green. "She didn't discover the body and had supposedly spent all morning in the cottage. When would she have seen his corpse?"

"Okay, let's say Marie is involved. Couldn't she have just, you know, killed him herself?" asked Sergeant Jones. "That's the simpler answer."

"Did you see her hands? That woman can barely hold a tissue, much less fire a gun," said Green. "Plus, if she had shot him, he would still be wearing his gloves. I think—"

Green's mobile rang, interrupting her thought. She fished it out of her pocket and rejoiced that it wasn't just another spam call. She answered briskly, "Inspector Green speaking."

She listened intently for a minute, then said, "Thanks, Kingsley, you're a star."

She turned back to Jones. "I texted Kingsley and asked her to take a look at the victim's brain. She found plaques in the brain characteristic of early Alzheimer's disease. That fits with my illness theory."

The inspector continued, "Let's go search the Cranstons' cottage and see what other evidence we can find. I suspect Marie will have laid a fire this morning, even though it's not particularly cold."

"Annabel, your leaps of logic are positively baffling," said Jones in disbelief.

Green responded, "Any mystery reader could have told you—the butler <u>always</u> did it."

Case #2:
The Cold Case

Chessingfield -- June

Sergeant Jones dropped a heavy cardboard box overflowing with papers onto Inspector Green's already cluttered desk.

"What's this?" asked Green, looking suspiciously at the pile of documents. She disliked all forms of paperwork and avoided them whenever possible.

"Part of Superintendent Young's cold case initiative," said Jones. "Remember? He announced it last week. Since it's been so slow, we've all been given an unsolved case. We're supposed to review the files and see if the investigating officers missed anything."

"Oh, I hate working old cases," said Green petulantly. "If you're lucky enough to track down any witnesses, they've forgotten everything by now. Plus, physical evidence is nonexistent. And there's no chance of CCTV footage. It's a waste of time."

"That's our Annabel, optimistic as ever!" said Jones. "I don't think the superintendent expects us to solve them all. I think it's more to keep us busy until the next case comes along."

He continued, "If it makes you feel better, I've been assigned a bank robbery from 1972. Both my prime suspect and my key witness are dead, and the bank doesn't exist anymore."

Green snorted and said, "Lucky you! The superintendent must have great faith in your powers of deduction." She eyed the box and concluded wearily, "I'll let you know if I have any success with this lot."

As Jones walked back to his desk, the inspector overturned the box and started sorting through the papers. Once they were in a reasonable semblance of order, she decided to start with the main case file. "KAYA BANERJEE – HOMICIDE – 18/8/2003" was printed in thick black ink on the front of the folder.

The inspector briefly thought back to August 2003. She had been with the police force in London for about six years and was still proving herself. She spent a lot of time directing traffic and her then-boyfriend wouldn't stop nagging her to get a "real" job.

She didn't miss those days one bit.

Inspector Green took a large sip of coffee, opened the folder, and started reading through the particulars of the case.

***

Kaya Banerjee had been murdered at her workplace, the Chessingfield Railway History Museum. Her throat had been slit and her body was found lying on a set of railroad tracks inside the building.

The museum had closed 20 minutes before the murder could have occurred, so the main suspects were Kaya's fellow employees. Three staff members were on the scene during the time of the murder, but none had heard or seen anything.

Although all three suspects had relatively weak alibis, the investigators were unable to determine any motive. They never recovered the murder weapon. After several months of fruitless interviews, the Dartshire police reluctantly shelved the case.

There were a number of photos in the file, and she took time to inspect each one.

First, a smiling photo of the victim at a birthday party several weeks before the murder. She was a pretty Indian woman with glossy black hair and a small gap between her two front teeth. Minimal makeup, minimal jewelry. She looked about the same age as the inspector was now—maybe late 40s or early 50s.

Second, a photo of Kaya's body as it was found, lying across a set of railway tracks. It reminded the inspector of old black-and-white movies with a woman tied to the tracks by a mustache-twirling villain. Her throat had been slit several times, so the front of the corpse was covered in blood. Not a very nice way to go.

Third, a photo taken of the main entrance to the Chessingfield Railway Museum. The ticket booth was on the left, and immediately behind that was a staircase leading to the office area. All full-time employees worked upstairs in a series of small offices.

On the right was a series of train cars, some on rails and some mounted on plinths. It was a huge museum, possibly a former warehouse, with rooms in the back housing special exhibits.

Fourth, the lead investigator had taken a photo of the three men on the scene when the body was discovered. No one was smiling, obviously.

All three men were wearing spotless, light blue train conductor dungarees—the uniform for all Railway History Museum employees. The back was labeled "L-R, Benson, Horowitz, Fanworth".

The inspector was grateful to have pictures to match the witness statements she was about to read. She liked to put a face to a name, and she wouldn't get the chance to meet these three suspects in person.

Oliver Benson was a classically handsome man: tall, symmetrical features, strong jaw. His blond hair was cut short on the sides, longer on the top. The museum's sky-blue uniform wasn't a particularly flattering outfit, but it suited him.

Joseph Horowitz had dark, curly hair and a serious face. Taller than Benson, his dungarees didn't quite reach his ankles. His arms were crossed, as if to protect himself from the camera. The inspector couldn't blame him. The man probably didn't wake up that day expecting to be suspected of murder.

Amos Fanworth was a full head shorter than the other two men. He was bald, with a bushy black beard that obscured the lower half of his face. Even in the long-sleeved train conductor uniform, you could see his arm muscles bulging through. He was powerfully built and gave the impression of a former rugby player.

The inspector laid the picture aside and started reading through the witness statements from the three men on the scene.

***

WITNESS STATEMENT #1 - OLIVER BENSON

My name is Oliver Benson and I'm the Operations Manager for the museum. I have worked here for the past six years, and I report to the General Manager, Kaya Banerjee.

I arrived at the museum around 8:30 this morning. I said hello to Amos, who was already in his office, and made a pot of coffee in the break room.

No one else had arrived. The museum opens officially at 10:00 a.m. and most of our office staff—that is, not the tour guides or the ticket-takers—arrive around 9:00.

Mondays are always a slow day for the museum, as far as attendance goes. Weekends are by far our busiest time. Our offices don't have windows facing the museum, so I don't know if there were any suspicious visitors today, but you can ask the ticket staff.

I stayed in my office working on a presentation until 10:30, when I went into the museum entrance area. We're having some new credit card readers installed at the entrance, so visitors don't have to pay in cash. I've been pushing for this upgrade for months. I met the vendor, gave him some instructions, and left as he got to work.

I ate a chicken sandwich for lunch at my desk. I didn't have any meetings until 1:00, when I met with Kaya in Meeting Room A to go over my estimates for next month's maintenance costs.

We have many trains on display. Most are immobile but one is operational, despite its old age. The train, a LMR 57 Lion, starts just inside the building and runs in a loop around the exterior of the museum. Visitors love it.

Kaya approved the figures and told me that she would pass them along to Amos. I then returned to my office, but I didn't walk straight there. I like to walk around the museum at least once a day to admire the trains. Each one is a marvel of 19th century engineering. That's why I took this job—it certainly wasn't the salary!

While I was walking through our exhibit on the 1840 Railway Regulation Act, I saw Joseph Horowitz half-crouching behind the LNER Class 4498 train. It almost looked like he was hiding from someone? He had a large package in his hand. I thought about walking up and asking him what was going on, but I decided against it. This would have been shortly after 2:00 in the afternoon.

Upon returning to my office, I started planning the logistics for a wedding that we'll be hosting in a few months. We've held many large events here in the past, but never a wedding ceremony, so it's an interesting challenge. I think this type of event will prove to be a great source of income for the museum.

I didn't leave my office from 2:15-5:00 p.m., except once to use the restroom. Joseph visited me around 3:00 to ask my opinion of a potential new hire. I didn't ask him what he was doing earlier, as it slipped my mind. It didn't seem potentially important until now.

Penny, our Sales Director, also stopped in around 4:00, just to chat. We talked a bit about Saturday's cricket match and her recent vacation to Switzerland.

A few minutes after 5:00, when the museum had closed and all of the visitors were gone, I left my office to perform one last task before heading home. As you might have noticed, I'm a jack of all trades around here.

It's been a few weeks since I last did basic maintenance on the LMR Lion, our functional locomotive, and I wanted to do it tonight so I wouldn't have to come in early tomorrow.

I shoveled some coal into the tender, greased up a few sticky joints, and scrubbed down the wheels. The process usually takes a little over 30 minutes, but it's worth it! I'm really proud of the old girl and I like to see her shining.

As I was working underneath the locomotive, someone walked by the train toward the place where Kaya's body was later found. I was focused on my task, but their presence registered in my mind. I couldn't really make out the shoes, but I would guess it was a man.

Around 5:30, I was scrubbing down one of the wheels when I heard someone shout "Oh my God!" in a panic. I didn't recognize the voice at first, but I dropped the cloth and ran across the museum to see what had happened.

I saw Amos standing next to Kaya's body, which was lying across the train tracks. As I arrived, Joseph ran down the stairs from his office. We were all stunned.

I was the only one with my mobile on me, so I called the police immediately. We moved away from the body and into the upstairs break room until the police arrived. To my knowledge, no one touched the body.

Kaya acted like her normal, efficient self today. She didn't seem nervous, or scared, or angry. I know you'll suspect Trevor, her husband, but their relationship seemed great. Miranda and I have gone out to dinner with them a few times over the past few years, and they always gave me the sense that they were deeply in love.

I cannot think of why anyone would do this to Kaya. She was a fantastic boss and a wonderful person. This is an absolute tragedy.

WITNESS STATEMENT #2 - JOSEPH HOROWITZ

My name is Joseph Horowitz. I joined the Chessingfield Railway History Museum three months ago as their new Human Resources Manager. It has been a pleasure working here, although I'm still learning the systems and processes. There's a lot that needs upgrading.

The team has been very welcoming. I would say it's a fairly tight-knit group, as most of them have worked together for years and everyone is a train enthusiast. Amos has a tattoo of a Stanier Coronation train on his right biceps, if you can believe it. I don't quite understand the fascination, myself.

Today was a completely normal day at the museum. I arrived a few minutes after 9:00 a.m. and went straight to my office. I responded to all of the messages in my inbox and went to Meeting Room B at 10:00 a.m. to conduct an interview. We're looking for a new Sales Coordinator and we've narrowed it down to three candidates. I thought this person, Greg Bassett, was very promising.

The interview ended around 11:00, then I escorted Greg out and took an early lunch. I walked down the street to Massimo's, a little Italian place that does meatball sandwiches. I ate there, alone, and returned to the museum a few minutes before noon.

I came back to my office, answered a few questions about our new time-off plan, and then Shelly Ramirez unexpectedly came into my office. She told me that one of her fellow tour guides, a man named Douglas French, had been increasingly hostile to her over the past few weeks. We talked through the issue and I promised to meet with him tomorrow.

During the afternoon, I left my office twice. Once to ask Oliver's opinion of Greg, and once to check July's payroll details with Amos. I waved at Kaya when I walked past her office, but we didn't really interact today. Our weekly 1x1 meeting is on Fridays, and she's a very hands-off manager. After that, I didn't leave my office until 5:30, when I heard Amos yell out.

I ran out of my office toward his voice and found him standing next to Kaya's body, which was lying across the tracks that lead out of the building, for our one operational train.

As I arrived, Oliver ran over from the other side of the museum. Amos appeared to be in shock. I asked him if he had seen anything, but he shook his head. I asked him if he had touched the body, he said no.

Oliver called 999, keeping an eye on Amos while I did a quick search for the perpetrator. I didn't find anyone hiding in the museum, but I checked the front door and it was unlocked. That must be how the killer got in, because the back door was bolted shut.

Oliver suggested that we should wait in the break room for the police to arrive, as we didn't want to disturb any evidence. I made a pot of tea and we sat there until the police arrived.

This has been one of the longest evenings of my life. Kaya's body… I'm never going to get that image out of my brain. She was covered in blood. I've never seen anything like it, and I never want to see anything like it again. I hope you find the killer soon.

WITNESS STATEMENT #3 - AMOS FANSWORTH

My name is Amos Fanworth. This has been a very upsetting day, but I will recount my actions to the best of my ability.

I woke up at 6:30, ate breakfast, and arrived at work at 7:30 a.m., which is typical for me. I like to get into the office and get a head start before the rest of the team arrives. I've been Accounting Manager at the museum over 12 years now, so I often get interrupted with questions. Having that extra time is very useful.

I worked in my office until 10:00 a.m., when I had my weekly update meeting with Kaya. Normally I wouldn't disclose this, but in light of what happened today, I think every detail is relevant. Kaya and I have become close friends during the time we've worked together, and she often confides in me.

Kaya has been having some trouble with her husband, Trevor. Over the past few years, his behavior has become increasingly erratic. He got a concussion during a football match in 2001 and she thinks the brain injury is causing his mood swings and angry outbursts. However, he refuses to see a doctor.

Over the weekend, Trevor got drunk at the White Swan and came home looking for a fight. Normally he calms down after a few minutes, but this time he actually punched a wall. It did more damage to his hand than the wall itself, but Kaya was very alarmed. She warned him that divorce was on the table.

She wanted my advice—should she stay if Trevor went to counseling, or should she officially start the separation process?

I'm going through a divorce myself, so I have a bit of experience there. I told her that if he's not willing to change himself, she can't change him. She said she was going to take a few days to think it over. They don't have kids, but they've been together almost two decades now. That's a lot to give up.

That meeting was supposed to take an hour but we ended up talking until about 11:45. Then I headed to the gym, because I always lift weights over my lunch break. I worked out for an hour, showered, and returned to the museum around 1:00.

I spent the afternoon at my desk, except one meeting at 3:00 to review last month's payroll details with Joseph. Our last HR manager ignored the financial side of things completely, so he's a breath of fresh air. I suspect he won't stay at the museum long after the events of today, though.

I normally leave the office at 4:30 p.m. sharp, but my soon-to-be-ex-wife Vanessa called my work line to discuss some specifics of the divorce settlement.

I will admit, it's not been the smoothest process. Neither of us are acting maturely at the moment. She wanted to change the custody schedule yet again, and she had some complaints about the division of assets.

I argued with Vanessa for about 30 minutes, then wrote my solicitor a long email summarizing the conversation and asking her advice. I packed up my things and walked toward the main entrance around 5:30.

We turn off the lighting for the exhibits when the museum closes, but we keep a few overhead lights on all night. It's dim in places, but you can see where you're going.

I saw something lying on the tracks as I started walking down the stairs. As I got closer, I realized that it was Kaya.

I know I yelled out, but the next few minutes are very hazy. Oliver says that's common when you have a traumatic experience. Joseph and Oliver both ran over, Oliver called 911, Joseph looked for anyone hiding in the museum.

We didn't want to disturb anything and I couldn't handle looking at Kaya's body, so we went upstairs to the breakroom to wait. We sat there in silence until the investigators came in.

This is such a senseless tragedy. I have lost a close friend and a great manager, and the world has lost a wonderful person.

***

"Well, I'll be damned," said Inspector Green, under her breath.

Jones immediately popped his head over the low wall separating their desks. "What is it? Did you spot something? Please save me from reading about the dullest bank robbery ever committed."

"I think so," said the inspector. "The lead detectives on this case did a thorough job, but they overlooked one vital clue."

What did the inspector notice?

HINTS

HINT #1:
Someone was lying about what he was doing
when the murder occurred.

HINT #2:
A picture is worth a thousand words—
specifically, the picture of the three suspects.

HINT #3:
Cleaning train engines is a messy job.

ANSWER

With excitement mounting in her voice, Green said, "You haven't read the files, but I'll summarize. The victim's throat was slit at the railway museum where she worked. It was messy. The killer didn't know what they were doing, and there was blood everywhere."

"Each of the three main suspects had a weak alibi. Each one was alone during the time of the murder, so no one could confirm their whereabouts. But Oliver Benson here said that he was cleaning engines and working under a locomotive when it happened."

She slid the photograph over to Jones and tapped her finger above Oliver's head.

"If he was telling the truth, he should be covered in grease and oil. Why is his uniform sparkling clean?" asked the inspector.

"Because he changed clothes at some point?" said Jones.

"Exactly. He had to change his outfit because it was covered in the victim's blood," said Green. "The other two work in HR and accounting, and it makes sense that their uniforms are spotless."

"Well, let's track down this Benson chap and see what he has to say for himself," said Jones. "There might not be any physical evidence left, but perhaps the guilt has been weighing on his conscience for the past 18 years."

***

It took the team a few days to track down Oliver Benson, who had changed addresses several times since 2003. He was now living in a hospice care center in east Chessingfield.

They were given permission to visit him, but the nurse in charge of the center warned them that he had, at most, weeks to live. His disease had advanced to the point where he might not be responsive to their questions.

The man lying in the bed was barely recognizable as the handsome man from the picture, as he was several stone lighter and had lost most of his hair. Oliver looked up and gave them a weak smile as they entered.

"What can I do for you, officers?" he asked, using the bed's electric controls to slowly maneuver the bed into an upright position.

"We're looking into the murder of Kaya Banerjee and we wanted to ask you a few questions," said Inspector Green.

"Wow, I'm impressed at the tenacity of our local police force," said Oliver with an ironic grin. "That was over 15 years ago. Don't you have more recent crimes to handle? Cyberbullying or something like that?"

"I don't like an unsolved mystery," said Green. "And I think you can help us there. Why did you lie about your alibi?"

Oliver's grin didn't waver. "I have no idea what you mean."

Green responded, "You said you were performing maintenance on the train during the time she was killed. But pictures from the investigation show that you didn't have a speck of grease, coal, or dirt on you when police arrived. What were you really doing?"

Oliver gazed at her for a few long seconds, then put his hands up in mock surrender. "If I wasn't a week away from meeting my maker, I would make something up. I've always been an excellent liar. But perhaps it's good for my soul to come clean, after all this time."

Green, saying nothing, looked at him expectantly.

"Yes, I killed her. I didn't want to, but she gave me no choice," he said. "She found out that I had been cheating on Miranda with our nanny. Cliché, I know, but Natasha was stunning and I couldn't resist the temptation."

"She was going to tell Miranda later that week. I couldn't risk losing my kids, and I was relying on Miranda's banking salary to stay afloat. I had expensive tastes back then, and the museum industry wasn't exactly lucrative."

Oliver leaned forward slightly, enjoying having an audience.

"I decided to try one last time to convince the high-and-mighty Kaya not to spill the beans, but I suspected it was futile. A smart man always has a backup plan," he continued.

"First, arrange a meeting with Kaya, making sure the front door was unlocked and that at least one other employee was on site at the time. Juries get confused by multiple suspects. You just need to introduce a sliver of reasonable doubt."

"I chose 5:30 on a Monday, as Joseph would be around. I knew the chances were slim that he would see anything. Our offices didn't have windows overlooking the exhibits. I completely fabricated the story about him hiding behind the train with a suspicious package. I wanted to point the investigators in his direction."

"Amos wasn't supposed to be there," continued Oliver. "He always leaves early. But, as he didn't interrupt, I was happy to have another suspect on site."

"I bought a carving knife from a charity shop over in Sterwood Chase a few days before. The conversation with Kaya went poorly, as I'm sure you guessed, and I was forced to cut her throat," said Oliver. "Not my finest moment."

"The LMS Royal Scot Class has a compartment on the side that's more or less invisible when closed. After making sure she was dead, I dropped it there. The cops searched the place high and low but they never found it. I'm sure the knife is still there to this day, as I didn't want to risk getting caught while removing it."

"Then I changed my clothes—I put the dungarees in the compartment as well—and returned to the train. I didn't want to be the one who found the body, so I waited there for a few minutes until I heard Amos yell. I felt a bit bad about that, because he was definitely traumatized for a few months there."

"Joseph got grilled by the investigators, as well as Kaya's husband Trevor," said Oliver. "Trevor didn't have an alibi, but there wasn't enough evidence to make charges stick. Joseph left the museum a few months later. As far as I know, Amos still works there."

He relaxed back into the bed. "And that's the end of my sordid tale. I regret very little. My marriage to Miranda fell apart a few years later, but I did well out of the divorce settlement. Maybe this illness is my punishment, but if so, it's long overdue."

"Now, if you don't mind," he said, reclining the bed back down, "I have some dying to do. Please see yourselves out."

Green and Jones looked at each other and walked out in disgust.

"That guy is a real piece of work," Jones said, shaking his head. "I can't say I'm sorry to see him go."

Inspector Green responded, "I'm just glad we can provide some closure to this case, even if justice won't be served."

Jones said, "Want to take the train back to the police station?"

Green said, "No, I think I'll walk. I've had quite enough of trains for one week."

Case #3:
The Perfect Alibi

Rosingham - July

Inspector Green knew, beyond a shadow of a doubt, who had murdered Jada Pritchett. She would bet her (admittedly meager) life savings on it. She wasn't going home—or going to sleep—until she could prove it.

"He did it, Jones!" said Green, visibly frustrated. "You don't spend 25 years on the force without developing a keen intuition about guilt and innocence!"

"I know he's the most likely suspect, and I don't like him either, but you keep ignoring one tiny problem," said Sergeant Jones. "He has a rock-solid alibi."

They sat across from each other in an empty interview room at police headquarters. It was just past 9:00 in the evening and both of them had grown tired and irritable. The remnants of their disappointing takeaway curry dinner sat, congealing rapidly, in the corner of the room.

"Let's go over the facts," said Inspector Green. "Start with what we know."

"Right. Jada Pritchett was kidnapped at 1:15 this afternoon," said Jones wearily. "There were no fewer than four eyewitnesses who saw a tall, masked man grab Jada off the street, bundling her into a dark blue van. Retired schoolteacher Emma Chorley immediately called the police."

"At the exact moment of the kidnapping, Harrison Langley was giving a presentation," said Green, rubbing her eyes.

"Yes, Harrison was running an online seminar about software marketing strategies," said Jones. "He lives alone in his flat, but there are dozens of attendees who can vouch that Langley was sitting in his home office from 1:00-2:00 p.m. today."

He continued, "Jada's kidnapping happened so quickly that none of the bystanders were able to intervene or to record the vehicle's number plate. Our team canvassed the area, but the search led nowhere."

"Until a few hours later, when the bartender of the Red Lion found her floating face-down in the canal behind the pub," said the inspector. "With her head bashed in."

"Yes, it was particularly nasty," said the sergeant. "Jada had put up quite a struggle and several of her nails were broken. Her purse, wallet, and phone were missing. Her face was mangled beyond recognition, but the sunflower tattoo on her shoulder was enough to identify her. We'll have the dental records by tomorrow morning."

"Okay. Jada was kidnapped at 1:15 and dead by 3:30 at the latest," said Green. "That implies that the kidnapper never intended to make ransom demands. He just wanted her dead, and quickly."

"And this took advance planning," replied Jones. "She kept a fairly regularly schedule, so he knew she would be walking down Newsom Street at that exact time. Unless it was a maniac killer who just grabbed the first person he saw."

The inspector gave him a withering look and said, "We can start speculating about serial killers tomorrow. Tonight, I want to focus on Harrison. The jealous ex-boyfriend. Obsessed with Jada. Angry at being dumped a few weeks ago. He's a narcissist who can't handle rejection and lashed out violently. It all fits."

"You keep ignoring his alibi!" said Jones hotly. "You can't just disregard something because it doesn't fit your theory! You always say that's the hallmark of a bad detective."

The inspector sighed and ran her fingers through her hair. "Okay, Jones. You've been very patient with me today. Let's watch the interview tape, then the video of Langley's presentation, and then we'll go home and get some sleep. Maybe inspiration will strike us in our dreams."

"That sounds good," said Jones, somewhat mollified. He opened the black laptop on the table, found the file, and pressed the "play" button in the right corner.

***

The interview room they were now sitting in came into focus. The camera was angled toward the suspect, so they could clearly see Harrison Langley's face. He was remarkably unperturbed, considering he was the prime suspect in a murder inquiry. He sat back in the hard wooden chair and looked at ease.

"Mr. Langley, we appreciate you coming in on such short notice," said Inspector Green. "And our condolences on your loss."

"Well, Jada and I broke up a few weeks ago, so I guess I wasn't going to be in her life much anyways," said Harrison coldly.

"She broke up with you, is that correct?" asked Sergeant Jones.

"Yes, we had been dating for over a year," said Harrison. "She came to my place the other day and said she wasn't in love with me anymore. I was upset at first, of course, but there are many more fish in the sea. I've already downloaded a few dating apps and the women of Rosingham are lining up."

Inspector Green looked at Harrison Langley and suspected that he didn't have much difficulty attracting women. He was well-built, with long dark hair and piercing green eyes. Not her type in the slightest, especially considering that his smile never reached his eyes. She noticed a small scratch on his right cheekbone.

"How'd you get that cut on your face?" asked the inspector.

"Oh, I was looking after a friend's cat a few days ago," said Harrison. "I tried to pet it, but it scratched me. It got my hand as well." He held up a bandaged hand.

"Cats are supposed to be good judges of character," said Green. "Do you have a lot of friends?"

"No. How is this relevant?" asked Langley, visibly annoyed.

Sergeant Jones changed the subject. "Can you think of anyone who might want to hurt Jada?"

"Not particularly," Harrison said. The investigators waited for more details, but he didn't elaborate further.

"We've looked through her phone records and it didn't seem like you were too happy about the breakup," said Green. "You sent some texts that sounded pretty threatening. How could you, you'll regret this, that sort of thing."

"I was drunk and upset," said Harrison. "Telling your ex-girlfriend that she'll regret leaving you isn't a crime, the last time I checked."

Green noted that throughout the interview, no matter who asked the question, Langley directed his answer to Jones. He had barely acknowledged her presence, although she was the lead investigator. 'Issues with women,' she thought to herself. 'We can use that.'

"Can you account for your movements this afternoon, Harrison?" asked Inspector Green.

"Yes. I was in my office all day, until your officers came to pick me up," said Langley. "I work from home."

"Were you alone the entire time?" asked Green.

"Yes, but I was giving a webinar from 1:00-2:00 and I was on a call with a customer from 4:00-5:00," said Harrison. "Between those two meetings, I had a headache so I took a nap. I assume that's not a criminal offense."

"So, you didn't drive anywhere today?" Green asked. "Do you have access to company vehicles in your line of work?"

"No, I didn't leave the house," said Harrison. "And I have a company credit card, but not a company car."

"Are you sure?" asked the inspector. "I thought women were beating down your door."

"Even a man of my stamina needs a break now and then," said Harrison with a smug smile. "And I do have a day job, you know."

"I bet they don't know about your history—one formal complaint of stalking and one restraining order," said Green. "Do you bring that up in conversation or is that not first-date material?"

"If you're going to keep questioning me, I think I'm going to need to call my solicitor," said Harrison, narrowing his eyes. "I'm starting to feel like a suspect."

"That's all for now. Thank you for your time, Mr. Langley," said Jones. "Please don't leave the area, as you might be called in for additional interviews."

Langley nodded and left the room without another word. Sergeant Jones hit "pause" and asked Inspector Green hopefully, "Well? Any flashes of brilliance?"

Green shook her head, lips tight.

"Well, let's watch his work presentation again," said Jones. He pressed play.

***

Harrison's smooth, oily voice filled their ears. "Thank you for joining me for today's webinar. Whether you work in app development, middleware, or services, the information I'll share over the next hour will help you take your marketing efforts to the next level."

The inspector, even less interested in the content of the presentation the third time around, scanned what was visible of Harrison's home office. She had yet to gather enough evidence to secure a search warrant of his flat.

Langley's office was bland and impersonal. The wall behind him was painted a dove gray. She could see the leaves of a ficus tree in the left corner. Although there was no artwork hanging on the wall, there was a modern black-and-white analog clock showing the time.

The clock had drawn her attention on her first viewing, but unfortunately the times aligned exactly with the stated webinar agenda. He started speaking at 1:00 p.m. sharp and finished at 2:01 that afternoon.

"CapEx models are becoming a burden on businesses who are looking to keep their assets in a flexible state. As a result, we see the market moving towards software-as-a-service models…"

She couldn't stay focused on the content and thought back to the interview. She should definitely reach out to both women he harassed in the past. Their testimony would be useful if the case came to trial.

"Both vendor and client are aligned towards mutual success based on adoption levels. This maintains flexibility for users while providing a predictable revenue stream for software providers…"

She was again struck by his good looks. He was a very attractive psychopath. As someone with dry, acne-prone skin since early adolescence, Inspector Green couldn't help noticing that his olive complexion was flawless. No freckles, no moles, no scars. She bet he used a whole suite of men's skin care products.

She reluctantly turned her attention back to Harrison's presentation. "Each strategy brings its own risks to your sales organization. First, you have to consider the transition of compensation, as new deals no longer provide the main revenue stream…"

Harrison was well-off financially and could have easily purchased a van in cash, without leaving a trail. Storing it, however, was another matter. His downtown apartment complex only allotted one car per tenant. She should send a team to look at nearby storage units.

"Second, you must factor in the churn in resources, as natural hunters are replaced by nurturers. This will cause…"

Perhaps he had an accomplice? Someone who kidnapped Jada while he established his alibi? Inspector Green shook her head slightly. Harrison didn't strike her as a very trusting person, and he said himself that he didn't have many friends.

"I'm afraid I've gone a bit over my allotted time, so we don't have time for a Q&A session today. Please send me any additional questions or comments you may have. My contact information is listed in the email you received this morning. Thank you very much for attending."

After the webinar ended, the video stopped and Inspector Green sat staring at the Dartford Police Department logo on the screen. She mentally reviewed her interview with Langley just a few hours earlier, then the content of the video. There must be something…

"Wait," said the inspector aloud. "WAIT."

She re-opened the video file, watched for a few seconds, and said to Sergeant Jones, "I think we've got him!"

How did the inspector know that Harrison's alibi was faked?

HINTS

HINT #1:
Harrison had planned the crime down to the last detail, but there was something he couldn't have foreseen.

HINT #2:
Harrison was tech-savvy.

HINT #3:
There was a difference in Harrison's appearance in the video and the interview.

ANSWER

"Langley recorded this presentation beforehand!" shouted the inspector triumphantly.

"What? How do you know? And, more importantly, can we prove it?" asked Jones.

"Look at his face!" said Green, pointing to the freeze frame. Harrison was caught mid-blink with his mouth open.

"I get it, he's an attractive bloke," said Jones grudgingly. "Though I wouldn't use this exact picture as his headshot."

"No, there's no cut on his face in this webinar!" said Green. "Langley said he got it from looking after a friend's cat a few days ago. If that was the case, why isn't it on his face during the presentation?"

"…because Jada scratched him today when he attacked her?" said Jones tentatively.

"EXACTLY. He couldn't have known that she would put up such a fight," said Green. "He kidnapped her during the day, knowing there would be witnesses on the scene. He planned the presentation for that exact time, giving him a perfect alibi."

"He purposefully made his presentation run long, so there was no chance of receiving questions from the audience," continued Green. "That means no actual interactions, but everyone attending the webinar would assume that he was presenting live."

"The clock on the wall was overkill, but he really wanted to hammer home that he was occupied during the time of the kidnapping," said Green.

"Between his lie about the cut and the threatening texts we found on Jada's phone, I think we have enough for a search warrant," said Green, with much satisfaction. "Maybe even an arrest. What do you think, Jones?"

Sergeant Jones said, "Let's go pick him up. I can't wait to see his face when break the news that his alibi wasn't up to scratch!"

Case #4:

Death at
Dartford House

Mansford -- August

Inspector Green had just ordered a bacon sandwich from her favorite café when her mobile rang. "Inspector Green speaking. What's up, Wilkes?"

Constable Wilkes responded breathlessly, "We just got a call from Rosingham. A man has been shot in the head! You need to head to the Dartford House Hotel right away."

He continued, "Sergeant Jones has secured the scene, and he'll debrief you when you arrive."

"Got it, thanks. Be there shortly," replied Inspector Green. She hung up, grabbed the sandwich, and set off for the hotel. Her mind was already buzzing. Another murder! Dartshire was becoming a hotbed of homicide.

Ten minutes later, the inspector stepped out of her car and surveyed her surroundings with a practiced eye. She had driven past the Dartford House Hotel many times before, but never given it a second thought.

The building was large but somewhat dilapidated, with chipped white paint and rotting wooden window frames. The surrounding grounds looked relatively well-maintained, but it was clear the property had seen better days.

She spotted Sergeant Jones waiting for her at the main entrance to the hotel. He flicked away his cigarette and smiled as she walked up.

"Ah, Annabel, glad you're here. This case is a doozy," said Jones. "Most of the evidence points to suicide, but there are a few things that suggest foul play."

"You always know how to get my attention, David," responded Green. "I'm hooked. Give me a rundown of what you've learned so far."

"I've yet to interview the suspects—wanted to wait until you got here—but here are the facts," replied Jones. "Mr. Albert Paulson, the owner of this fine establishment, was found dead in his office earlier today."

He continued, "Mr. Paulson was slumped forward over his desk with a small black handgun clutched in his right hand. The bullet entered his right temple, which suggests suicide, but our crime scene analysts have yet to discover a note. He had no history of depression and didn't tell anyone that he planned to end his life."

"Interesting," said the inspector. "Was his office locked, by any chance?"

"No such luck," said Jones. "The large window behind his desk was wide open and his office door was unlocked, so anyone could have let themselves inside. There was no sign of a struggle, though."

Jones continued, "Fortunately, the hotel's six guests the previous evening all checked out early this morning, and there haven't been any deliveries or other visitors to the hotel. That means we only have four viable suspects, if it was murder."

"Oh, that's excellent news," said Inspector Green. "You know nothing makes me happier than a limited suspect pool. Let's go see what they have to say for themselves."

***

The responding officers had helpfully kept all of the suspects separated, so none had seen or spoken to each other since the discovery of the body at noon. The chef was in the kitchen, the receptionist in the lobby, the groundskeeper in the backyard, and the handyman in the basement.

She started with the owner's daughter, Chelsea Paulson, who also worked as the hotel's receptionist. She was an attractive woman in her early thirties with a blonde pixie cut. Chelsea's green cotton dress complemented her eyes— which, the inspector noted, showed no sign of recent crying.

Inspector Green said, "I'm so sorry for your loss, Ms. Paulson. How are you feeling?"

"It all feels a bit surreal," said Chelsea, absentmindedly rubbing her neck. "I think it's going to take a while to sink in."

"Had your father been behaving strangely recently?" asked Jones. "Was he concerned about money?"

"No, he was his normal cantankerous self," said Chelsea. "That's what makes this so hard to believe. I spent a few years volunteering as a grief counselor for teens, so I'm familiar with suicide warning signs. He didn't give any indication that he was about to kill himself."

"Can you tell us about your movements this morning? Specifically, between 9:00 and noon?" asked Green.

"The last guests checked out of the hotel around 9:30 a.m. and no one was scheduled to arrive until 3:00, so I had the morning off," Chelsea said. "I walked into town and got a haircut at Betty's Salon. I'm donating eight inches of hair to a charity that makes wigs for children with cancer."

"Around 10:45, I came back to the hotel and read a book on the veranda. Our groundskeeper Tom was mowing the lawn, so it was pretty loud, but I don't mind background noise. Sometimes I feel like it actually helps me concentrate better, you know?"

"What were you reading?" asked Jones.

"I've just started a biography of Joan of Arc," said Chelsea. "It's very interesting so far."

She continued, "I didn't go back inside the hotel until a few minutes before noon. I walked straight to Mr. Paulson's office to let him know lunch was ready and found him dead!"

"I saw the gun in his hand and I could tell he was dead from the doorway. I grabbed my mobile phone and called the police immediately, then waited in the lobby until the officers arrived."

Inspector Green looked up from her notepad. "I notice you called your father Mr. Paulson. Is that how you usually referred to him?"

Chelsea's lips tightened. "Yes. Ever since I was a young girl, he preferred me to call him that, rather than dad or daddy," she said, with a hint of sadness in her voice. "He wasn't very emotionally demonstrative towards me or my mother. She passed away when I was nine."

Sergeant Jones and Inspector Green made eye contact. Clearly, Chelsea had a complicated relationship with her father. However, time was ticking away, and the inspector decided to keep the initial interview short and move to the next suspect.

***

The detectives walked through the hotel restaurant, then into the kitchen to speak with the chef, Liam Adelson. Liam was a tall man in his early thirties, slightly balding, with close-set eyes. He was wearing a spotless white chef's coat.

"Hello, Mr. Adelson," said the inspector. "We'd like to ask you a few questions regarding the death of Mr. Paulson. You're aware he was shot in his office this morning?"

Liam surveyed the inspector suspiciously before saying brusquely, "Yes, the constable shared the news before telling me to stay put in the kitchen. But I'm not going to pretend that I'm sad Albert is dead. He was a thoroughly unpleasant man who bullied us all, even his own daughter."

"Chelsea is a wonderful girl who deserves much better treatment. I don't know how such an awful man produced such a gorgeous woman..." He trailed off, aware that his response had taken a personal turn.

Inspector Green nodded without comment and redirected Liam by asking about his morning's activities.

"I spent all morning working in the kitchen. I was here from about 10:00 a.m. to a few minutes after noon. I was just about to bring out lunch when your sergeant walked in and told me what had happened."

"What did you make for lunch?" asked the inspector, hoping her rumbling stomach wasn't audible. She really should have eaten that bacon sandwich on the drive over.

"I made venison pies, mashed potatoes, sauteed green beans, and sticky toffee pudding for the five of us," said Liam.

"Normally I don't go to so much effort when we don't have any lunch bookings, but we have a wedding next weekend and I wanted to test out the menu."

"Obviously, no one ate anything after your sergeant told us the news. I couldn't leave the kitchen and I had to chuck it all in the bin. Such a waste," he said, gesturing toward the rubbish container behind him.

"What do you think happened?" asked the sergeant.

"It's suicide, ain't it?" Liam replied. "He must have done it while I was making lunch, otherwise I would have definitely heard the shot. My kitchen isn't far from Mr. Paulson's office, but it gets incredibly loud in here."

"Between the microwave, the blender, the dishwasher, and things sizzling on the stove, I can't even hear myself think," he finished.

"Are you going to continue working at the hotel?" asked Jones.

"I don't see why not," said Liam. "It all depends on what Chelsea decides to do with the place. If she sells, I'll probably go stay with my brother in Sydney for a few months. I think Australia would suit me."

Inspector Green and Sergeant Jones thanked Adelson, then walked outside to speak with the groundskeeper.

***

They found Thomas Warner on the other side of the hotel grounds, trimming an overgrown privet hedge. He looked up, smiled, and put down his gardening shears.

Thomas was a handsome young man in his mid-twenties with messy brown hair and a lopsided smile. His grass-stained cargo pants and blue T-shirt were both in desperate need of a wash.

The detectives introduced themselves, and Thomas responded with enthusiasm.

"I've never been involved in a real murder investigation before!" he said. "My mum watches all the crime shows on the BBC. She's going to be beyond chuffed that I'm being interviewed. Go on, grill me!"

Green bit back a smile and asked, "What was Albert Paulson like to work for?"

"Mr. Paulson was... not the nicest man," said Thomas. "He was also incredibly cheap when it came to hotel upkeep. 'Penny wise and pound foolish,' as my Gran would say."

"I met with him around 10:00 this morning to try to convince him to remove a tree in the parking lot. It died last summer and it's starting to rot, so it's only a matter of time before a branch falls on someone's car and we have a lawsuit on our hands."

"Mr. Paulson wouldn't hear of it, though," Thomas continued. "I admit, my temper got the best of me and I told him that he was being a short-sighted idiot. He told me to get out of his office before he sacked me. But I swear, I didn't kill him!"

"No one is saying you did," said Inspector Green reassuringly. "Tell me about your movements this morning."

"I had breakfast at home before heading to work around 9:00. My first task was watering the flowers in the front and back beds. It's been a hot summer so they're quite thirsty lately. That took about an hour."

"I went to Mr. Paulson's office around 10, as I said. I left the office around 10:15 and headed to the garden shed to get the lawn mower and my other equipment," said Thomas. "I spent the rest of the morning mowing the lawn. I usually wear earplugs to protect my hearing, so while I'm out mowing grass, I'm pretty much deaf. I'm sorry I can't be more helpful!"

"Did you see Chelsea?" asked the inspector.

"See Chelsea? Did someone say I was seeing Chelsea?" stammered Thomas, quickly turning red. "I'm not. I mean, I would love to date Chelsea, she's a stunner, but I've never made a move."

The inspector replied gently, "No, I meant did you see Chelsea out on the veranda? She said she was outside, reading a book there this morning."

Thomas said, "Oh. Right. No, I didn't notice her there but I wasn't looking around. I'm in my own world when I mow the lawn. It's almost like meditation."

Inspector Green asked, "Do you own a gun? Are you aware of any guns located on the hotel premises?"

"No, we don't have any firearms here," said Thomas. "We don't have any major issues with wild animals and there's never been a reason to keep them. Even if we did, I'm a gardener. I don't know how to shoot."

Sergeant Jones asked, "If the hotel closes, what are your plans?"

"Well, I was approached recently by a landscape architecture firm in Mansford," said Thomas. "I'm only about halfway through the interview process, but if that goes well, that's my next step."

"We'll let you know if we have any further questions," said Inspector Green. "How did this compare to the police interviews on TV?"

"If I'm honest, it was a bit too gentle," said Thomas with a smile. "Next time, you'll have to bring me into the station and shine a bright light into my eyes."

***

Green and Jones re-entered the hotel and headed downstairs to the last interview of the day. Harold Ruffin, the handyman, was a burly man over six feet tall. He had short red hair and a matching mustache. He was wearing loose-fitting jeans, a gray T-shirt, work boots, and a heavy tool belt around his waist.

"Mr. Ruffin, we'll make this interview as quick as possible," said Inspector Green. "At any point this morning, did you hear a gunshot?"

"I didn't hear anything that sounded remotely like a gunshot," said Harold. "Though that's not surprising. I spent all morning down here in the basement, trying to fix a leak."

"I'm not a plumber but I do a little of everything around here: carpentry, roofing, electrical work, you name it. I do my best to keep this place running, but between you and me, the hotel is falling apart. I've been begging old Paulson to hire additional help, but he won't hear of it."

"You were in the basement all morning?" asked the inspector.

"Yeah, from just after nine until whatever time the police officer came down here to share the bad news," replied Harold. "Though... can I be honest with you? The bad news wasn't that bad."

He continued, "I don't like to speak ill of the dead, but Paulson was a nightmare. He treated everyone like garbage and the hotel has suffered for it. I hope that Chelsea sells this place and moves on to bigger and better things."

Inspector Green, sensing the tender note in his voice, asked Harold about his relationship with Chelsea Paulson.

"I don't need to be under oath to tell you that I think Chelsea is the perfect woman," said Harold shyly. "She's always been a beautiful, kind soul. She's so stunning, even with that short haircut. Now that she's out from under the old man's thumb, I might finally ask her out. I've been thinking about it for years."

Green and Jones shared a brief look, both thinking that Harold Ruffin was going to have a lot of competition there.

"Do you own a gun?" asked the inspector.

"No, I've never much cared for guns," said Harold. "My cousin Winston was a regular hunter until he accidentally shot off his big toe. I steer clear of the things."

"What are your plans now?" asked Jones.

"Well, if the place stays open, I'll stay and help Chelsea out," said Harold. "With a little bit of love, the hotel could return to its former glory. If she decides to get rid of it, I'll probably go back to school and get my degree. I had to drop out of university when my dad got sick, and it's something I've always wanted to do."

"Thank you for your cooperation, Mr. Ruffin," said Green. "Now that we've spoken with everyone present during the time of the murder, you're free to wait in the hotel restaurant. We will release you shortly."

***

Inspector Green and Sergeant Jones then moved into the hotel's small conference room to discuss their findings.

"One thing's for certain: no one seems very upset about Mr. Paulson's death. I assume that Chelsea inherits the entire estate?" asked Inspector Green.

"Yes, Constable Wilkes checked the will and Mr. Paulson left everything to Chelsea," replied Sergeant Jones. "Despite the state of Dartford House, the land itself is quite valuable. She could easily get a few million pounds for it. And all three men seem to be in love with her, so that's a motive for each of them."

"Well, I know at least one person has lied to us," said Inspector Green. "Let's start there and see where that line of questioning takes us."

Who was lying?

HINTS

HINT #1:
Mr. Paulson was definitely alive when the groundskeeper left his office.

HINT #2:
It's important that none of the suspects claimed to have seen each other after breakfast.

HINT #3:
Chelsea Paulson had never cut her hair that short before.

ANSWER

"Jones, could you go to the dining room and fetch Harold Ruffin?" asked Inspector Green.

Sergeant Jones nodded, left the room, and promptly returned with the handyman. The inspector noted that Harold's breathing had quickened. Good, she thought. He was losing his nerve.

"I appreciate you coming in again, and I won't keep you very long," said the inspector. "I had one follow-up question after our conversation. You didn't leave the basement all morning? Not even to use the restroom?"

Harold swallowed hard. "No ma'am, I was down there for hours and didn't leave once. As I said, I was trying to fix that plumbing issue."

Inspector Green smiled faintly. "Then can you tell us how you knew that Chelsea had her hair cut short? She went to the salon around 10:30. You shouldn't have crossed paths."

Harold's eyes darted back and forth between the two officers. "Um, she must have told me that she was going to get it done. And I just assumed that it would look good. Since she's a beautiful woman. Yeah."

"Here's what I think happened," said Inspector Green. "I think you reached your limit with old Mr. Paulson. Maybe it was his mistreatment of Chelsea, his neglect of this property, his refusal to increase your wages, or a combination of all three. You had enough."

"I don't think this murder was premeditated. You had an argument and shot him in his office around 11:00. When you were sneaking through the hotel back to the basement, you glanced through the window and spotted Chelsea sitting on the veranda. That's when you saw her hair."

"I… I don't know what you're talking about," said Harold. He licked his lips and attempted a smile. "I was down here all day."

"When I do a background check, I'm not going to find that you own a small handgun, despite what you told us? And I won't find a gun or a silencer in that toolbelt you're wearing?" asked Inspector Green.

"Yes, okay?! Yes," growled Harold. "I killed him. But ask anyone, that man was a monster! I had to get him out of the way. For Chelsea, for me, for the greater good of humanity!"

Sergeant Jones calmly grabbed his handcuffs and placed them on an unresisting Harold. The inspector felt a keen sense of satisfaction as Harold was led away. They would have caught him eventually based on the gun records, but there was something extremely gratifying about an immediate solve.

The inspector headed back to her car, where she found the bacon sandwich, now cold and thoroughly unappetizing. Her stomach rumbled. It had been a long day.

Jones knocked on the inspector's driver-side window and she rolled it down.

"Fancy a pub dinner?" he asked. "We can finish the paperwork over a platter of fish and chips."

"That sounds excellent, and I think we've earned it," Green responded. "Solving a murder really works up the appetite!"

Case #5:
History Repeats Itself

Sterwood Chase -- September

"Come on, Annabel," said Sergeant Jones, as the detectives drove along the motorway. "If you could travel back in time, where would you go? We're going to a history museum, after all."

"The more I learn about the past, the more I'm grateful to be born in the 20th century," said Inspector Green. "Life wasn't great before electricity, indoor plumbing, and antibiotics. Everyone died early and smelled awful."

"Aw, you're no fun," said Jones. "I would go back to Tudor times and go hunting with King Henry VIII. I want to eat a 14-course meal that's mostly meat."

"You want to visit a man whose enduring legacy is cutting people's heads off?" asked Green incredulously. "You're braver than I thought. Or you watch too much television."

Jones ignored that and changed the subject. "I haven't been to the Sterwood Living History Museum in ages. I went there every year as a kid. Wouldn't have guessed that a murder would be the reason for my next visit."

The Sterwood Living History Museum showcased what life was like for American pioneers in the early 1800s. The museum's founders had salvaged a variety of US buildings from the time period and arranged them around a large central square.

Each building housed an actor who described an aspect of daily life and answered visitors' questions. The museum offered classes on cheesemaking, woodworking, embroidery, and other 19th-century must-have skills.

Inspector Green said, "What do we know so far about the case?"

The sergeant flipped open his notebook and read aloud. "The museum's current owner, Stuart Jordan, was found lying face-up in the middle of the main square. His body was discovered by his wife at 9:45, 15 minutes before the museum's opening time, and she immediately called the police."

Jones continued, "He had been stabbed through the chest with something huge. The weapon has yet to be recovered, but we've got a search team actively working on it."

They pulled into the parking lot and spotted Constable Brittany Hedges, drinking a large cup of coffee near the main entrance.

She beckoned them over and said, "Glad to see you both. We don't have much to go on at the moment, but you've developed quite the reputation for spotting things that others miss."

"Shall we start with the body?" asked the inspector.

"Absolutely. Follow me," the constable replied.

***

They walked through the museum gates and soon found themselves in the main square. It was abuzz with activity, from analysts picking fibers off the dead man's jacket with tweezers to crime scene photographers taking pictures from every angle.

Even without a medical degree, the inspector could tell that Mr. Jordan was dead from 20 feet away. There was a gaping hole in his chest and his limbs were splayed out on the ground at unnatural angles.

They walked closer and she bent over the corpse for a better look.

"Whatever he was stabbed with, it must have been enormous," said Inspector Green. "I could roll a bowling ball through his torso."

"I'll say," responded Constable Hedges. "At least two feet long, likely bigger, and seven inches in diameter. Based on the flesh surrounding the injury, the weapon was smooth, not serrated."

She continued, "I assumed we would find the murder weapon in no time, but we've torn this place apart. We even conducted body searches of everyone on the premises, on the off chance they were hiding a sharpened battering ram in their old-timey petticoats. But no luck."

"Interesting," replied the inspector. "Have the crime scene analysts spotted any footprints around the corpse, or other evidence left behind on the victim's body?"

"Not yet," said the constable. "But it's still early days. In the meantime, do you want to speak to our suspects?"

"Yes, I want to know more about our victim and why someone might choose to kill him in such a violent fashion," said Inspector Green. "This murder feels… personal."

"We have four primary suspects," said the constable. "The first officers on the scene were admirably efficient. They cordoned off the entrance immediately so that no visitors could wander in. They also reviewed the security footage from the cameras placed around the perimeter, which show no one entering or leaving during the relevant time period."

"Why does this museum have security cameras?" asked Sergeant Jones. "Surely, there's not much here worth stealing, unless you have a fondness for vintage quilts."

"Mr. Jordan had them installed a few months ago," replied the constable. "According to his wife, he had started becoming paranoid about safety. She doesn't know why."

"This case becomes more interesting by the minute," said the inspector. "Well, Jones, let's make the rounds and see what we can dig up."

***

Their first stop was the Bachmann Family Barn, which had been built in 1801. It was a large building that smelled strongly of straw. The inspector guessed that the search team had already visited, as the bales of hay were scattered haphazardly and all the crates had been pulled off the shelves.

They walked in and spotted Daisy Beecroft, a young woman with pale blonde hair. She was petite, but her arms showed unexpected strength as she churned butter furiously. She was grimly focused on her task and didn't notice them right away.

"Ms. Beecroft?" said Sergeant Jones. She looked up, wiped away her hair with the back of her hand, and nodded mutely. "We'd like to ask you a few questions."

Daisy led them to a few bales of hay in the corner and they all sat down. She cleared her throat and asked in a wavering voice, "So what can I do for you?" The inspector noticed that her eyes were red-rimmed.

"We won't take up much of your time, as we know you've had a shock," said the inspector. "First, how long have you known Stuart Jordan?"

Daisy took a deep breath and responded, "I met Mr. Jordan five years ago. This was my first job after I graduated from university, and I've been here ever since. I do auditions for proper acting jobs on the side, but nothing has panned out yet."

"I give tours of the barn," she went on. "I also do some demonstrations, like making butter and goat cheese. Normally I wait until visitors have arrived before I start churning the butter, but I just needed something to do. I feel so useless right now." She picked a piece of straw off her dress and dropped it on the ground.

Her voice resumed wavering as she continued. "Stuart was always very kind to me. He supported my acting career wholeheartedly when other people, including my own mother, told me to give up. He was basically my mentor. And now he's dead! What am I going to do?" She dissolved into sobs.

Sergeant Jones patted her awkwardly on the back and proffered a tissue, which she accepted. The inspector waited a moment and continued, "Only two more questions before we let you get back to work. First, can you think of anyone who might have a reason to harm Mr. Jordan?"

"No!" said Daisy quickly. "No one in the world! He was such a gentle soul. A very loving man." She bit her lip.

"Last question. Where were you between 8:30 and 10:00 a.m. today?"

"I arrived around 8:00 and was here in the barn the entire morning," said Daisy. "I like to come in here and read before my shift starts. This place is much more peaceful than my flat. My next-door neighbor likes to practice her clarinet at all hours."

She pointed over at an open book, face-down on a nearby bale of hay. "I ate a granola bar for breakfast and read *Wuthering Heights* until I heard Mrs. Jordan scream. I then ran out and saw the body and…"

She started weeping again and the inspector took pity on her, quietly moving out of the barn to the next suspect.

"I learned nothing from that," said the sergeant. "Wait, that's not entirely true. I learned that there are still people who read *Wuthering Heights* for fun."

"Well, I thought it was an interesting conversation," replied the inspector. "Let's see what the victim's wife has to say."

***

They met Mavis Jordan in the main office, near the museum entrance. As they walked in, Mavis slammed shut a metal filing drawer. The room was full of filing cabinets and her desk was blanketed in papers, about two inches deep. It was not a very tidy space.

Mavis Jordan was an intimidating woman. Although she was of short stature and very thin, she managed to radiate a sense of power. She fixed the inspector with a cool, appraising glance. Inspector Green could tell immediately that Mrs. Jordan was used to being in charge.

"Well, let's get this over with," Mavis snapped. "You people have already ransacked my office looking for the murder weapon. What do you want to know?"

"We'll be as quick as possible, as we know you've suffered a great loss," responded the inspector soothingly. "First, please tell me about your relationship with your husband."

"Our relationship? Ha! At first, I considered lying to you. But I'm not a good liar, and I don't think there's any use. Our marriage has been in trouble for years, Inspector. I can't put an exact date on it, but roughly when that little tramp showed up."

"And by little tramp, you mean…" prodded the inspector.

"HER! Daisy! She shows up here, all fresh-faced and wide-eyed, and my husband fell for her. They think they've fooled me, but I know what they've been up to for the past few years," said Mavis with a sneer.

"Neither of them was good at hiding the relationship. It just wasn't convenient for me to confront Stuart about it. I can live with him having a mistress," she concluded sharply.

"Can you think of anyone who may have had a reason to kill your husband?" asked Inspector Green. "Someone with a grudge, perhaps?"

"I've been thinking about it since the second I found his body," she said. "I mean, it could have been Daisy. Maybe he broke things off with her. Or maybe it was Richard. He was unhappy that Stuart was considering selling the museum to investors. It could even have been Eddie. I heard them yelling at each other yesterday, but I couldn't make out what the argument was about."

"Tell me more about your movements this morning," said the inspector.

"I was here, in this office, starting around 7:30 this morning," said Mavis. "I like to get an early start, though the museum doesn't open until 10:00. I don't know where Stuart was. I left the house before he was even awake."

"A little after 9:40, I walked out into the courtyard and saw Stuart lying there. I screamed, everyone came running, and as soon as I regained my wits, I called the police. And that's the truth." She scowled at both police officers defiantly.

"Thank you for your time, Mrs. Jordan. We'll be in touch if we have any follow-up questions," said the inspector.

"Yikes, that is one terrifying woman," said Sergeant Jones after they left the office.

"Yes, she certainly puts up a tough exterior," responded the inspector. "But I wonder if there isn't more to her than that. Let's go find out how angry Richard was about the sale of the museum, shall we?"

***

Richard Fullom worked in the Johnston Smithy, originally constructed in 1808. The forge was enormous, and the inspector was impressed by the dizzying array of chains, banister poles, ornamental fire pokers, and knives on the walls.

It was extremely hot in the forge, as the fire was roaring. They found Richard at his anvil, banging away on a square piece of metal. There was a large pile of identical metal squares on the ground next to his feet.

"Hello, Mr. Fullom," shouted the inspector over the loud clangs. "Could you take a break? We need to ask you a few questions."

Richard put down his hammer and faced the investigators. He gave them a small smile. "Ask away. I'm happy to help."

"What's that you're making?" asked Inspector Green. She found that simple questions about a suspect's hobby often loosened them up.

"Oh, this?" replied Richard. "I'm instructing an advanced blacksmithing course tomorrow—that is, if it isn't canceled due to what happened today—and we're making iron chest hinges."

He continued, "I came in early today to make a bunch of samples to show the class. Usually, I don't get here until 10:00 on the dot when the museum opens. I'm not an early riser."

"Interesting. And is it always scorching in here?" asked Green, wiping her forehead with the back of her hand.

Richard smiled. "I'm afraid it's a bit toasty when the forge is running. And it's warm for September, which doesn't help." He leaned against the brick wall and crossed his arms.

"I'd like to get a better sense of your relationship with Mr. Jordan. How long have you known him?" asked the inspector.

"Stuart hired me almost a decade ago to run the museum's blacksmithing operations and it's been a dream job," said Richard. "I owe him so much. But I didn't know him very well on a personal level. We only interacted here at the museum."

"Did Mr. Jordan have any enemies that you're aware of?" replied the inspector. "Clearly, someone wanted him out of the picture."

"I can't think of anyone who might do him harm," said Richard. "The museum was doing okay financially, and he didn't have any business rivals. I mean, he and Mavis fought a fair amount, but don't all married couples? And he and Eddie had regular dust-ups, but they're old friends and it was all bluster."

"What about Daisy Beecroft? Would she have any reason to kill Mr. Jordan?" asked Jones.

"Sweet Daisy? I don't think so," responded Robbins. "I think that she was in love with him, though. I don't have a shred of evidence, but every time they were in the same room, she couldn't take her eyes off him."

"Another witness told us that you were angry that Stuart Jordan was considering selling this property," said the inspector, watching Richard closely. "Can you tell us more about that?"

"Of course," said Richard. "A development company had offered Mr. Jordan a staggering amount for the land. They wanted to build a bunch of high-rise condominiums."

"It would have been a ridiculous thing to construct here, and I told Mr. Jordan as much," said Richard. "I'm sure he wasn't seriously considering the offer. And now that Mrs. Jordan is in charge, she'll never sell. She loves this place even more than I do."

"One last question before you get back to work, Mr. Fullom," said the inspector. "Can you account for your movements between 8:30 and 10:00 a.m. today?"

"Like I said, I was here all morning," replied Richard. "I got here around 8:30, and I was alone the whole time. Maybe someone heard me clanging away and can vouch for me."

The inspector thanked him for his time and they left the forge, grateful to be back outside in the fresh air.

"Who's your money on, Inspector?" asked the sergeant. "So far, I still think Mavis did it. I wouldn't want to be on her bad side."

"Now, Jones, you know I like to interview everyone before I start flinging accusations around!" said the inspector with a smile. "Let's go speak with Eddie and see what their fight was about."

***

They crossed the courtyard to the Branson Courthouse, built in 1802. It was a lovely stone building with large pillars that must have taken a staggering amount of effort to relocate.

Eddie Girdlestone was a rotund, middle-aged man with thinning black hair. He looked up expectantly from behind the judge's seat and smiled at the detectives. He had a gap between his two front teeth that made him look younger than his age.

"I'm glad you're here," said Eddie. "I've been antsy all morning and I want to help in any way that I can. But I don't know how much help I'll actually be. I got here a few minutes before Mavis screamed."

"We appreciate your cooperation," said the inspector. "We'll get straight into it. Someone has told us that you and Stuart Jordan had an argument yesterday. Can you tell me what that was about?"

The color drained from Eddie's ruddy face. "So, you've heard about that. I guess I had better be completely upfront. I've known Stuart for almost 20 years now, and I would call him both a boss and a friend. I'm always honest with him about what I think."

He swallowed and continued. "Basically, I wasn't pleased with the way he was treating Ms. Beecroft. You probably already know that the two of them had a secret relationship. I feel like almost everybody in Sterwood Chase knows at this point."

"But I thought he was taking advantage of her, and I told him as much. I mean, she's got to be 20 years younger than he is! And she's besotted with him, even though he treats her badly. He wouldn't listen. I'm not proud of what I said to him, especially now that he's gone."

"Stuart was still very dear to me, despite his recent behavior," continued Eddie. "I would never lay a finger on him. And I have no idea who else would, honestly. This all seems like a terrible dream."

"Where were you before arriving at work?" asked the inspector.

"At my house," Eddie responded. "I live alone. I woke up, ate a quick breakfast, walked my dog Skipper around the block, and got here a little after 9:00 this morning."

"I went straight to the courthouse to prepare for this weekend's mock trial," he continued. "We're going to re-enact the 1807 treason trial of Aaron Burr. I had been in the courtroom only a few minutes when I heard the scream."

"It was a bit faint, as these stone walls are thick, but I went outside to see what the racket was about. I thought maybe someone was playing a prank. I wish it had been a prank," Eddie said.

"That's all the questions we have for now. Thank you for your assistance, Mr. Girdlestone," said the inspector. "We'll be in touch."

***

The two detectives headed to a nearby restaurant to eat a late lunch and discuss their findings. Inspector Green chewed her sandwich, deep in thought. After a few minutes, Jones broke the silence.

"As far as I can tell, no one said anything particularly incriminating," said Sergeant Jones, with frustration in his voice. "No one has a decent alibi for the morning. But also, no one has a motive that stands out to me! Maybe the wife? But she clearly knew about the affair for years, so why kill him now?"

Jones took a large bite of hamburger. His phone buzzed and he looked down at the glowing screen as Green responded.

"In this specific case, I think that motive is irrelevant," said Green. "What matters is finding the murder weapon."

"Some news on that front. We just got a text message from the head of the search," Jones said, holding up his phone. "They haven't found a single item that could have produced that injury. They scoured the grass for signs of recent digging, but no luck. And, obviously, they checked every knife and sharp object in the forge. Nothing matches."

"Without the murder weapon, we don't have much to go on," Jones concluded. "It's starting to feel a bit hopeless."

"Don't worry, Jones," replied the inspector. "I've been thinking things over, and I have a good idea of what happened to the murder weapon, after all."

How did the killer hide the murder weapon?

HINTS

HINT #1:

The weapon that killed Stuart Jordan is no longer in its original form.

HINT #2:

The murder weapon was out in plain sight while the detectives were interviewing the suspects.

HINT #3:

The murder weapon was melted down.

ANSWER

"Well?" said Jones. "Where is it?"

Inspector Green just looked at him expectantly.

"You are the worst," said Jones. "Please enlighten me, oh great and wondrous genius. You put Sherlock Holmes to shame. You make Hercule Poirot cry himself to sleep at night. Miss Marple retired because she knew she couldn't compare to you. Are you satisfied?"

"That flattery was adequate," said Inspector Green with a broad smile. "You deserve to hear my theory."

"Let's start by eliminating the places our search team has already checked. It's not buried in the courtyard or the surrounding grounds. It's not in the barn. It's not in the filing cabinets of the office. It's not in the courthouse. And none of the suspects had the opportunity to leave the museum and dispose of it."

"You forgot the forge. It's not in the forge," added Jones.

"That's where you're wrong, my friend," said the inspector.

"What?" spluttered Jones, choking slightly on his soda. "They checked all of the weapons in the forge and not a single one matched the injury on the victim."

"Of course they didn't match," said the inspector. "Richard isn't stupid. He's been planning this murder since the day he heard that Stuart Jordan wanted to sell the museum."

"I'm going to need more details," said the sergeant. "Immediately."

"My suspicions were first aroused by the irregular size and shape of the murder weapon," said the inspector. "Like Constable Hedges said earlier, it was basically a sharpened battering ram."

"It doesn't seem like something that would be easy to buy in a shop. But you could certainly make it, with access to enough material."

"A good start," said Jones. "Go on."

"Once you've committed a murder, especially with an unusual implement, you need to get rid of the weapon as soon as possible," continued Green. "Again, the blacksmith has the best opportunity to do so. He could easily melt down the weapon in his forge."

"What I think happened: Richard heard about the potential sale. Not wanting to lose his dream job, he asked Stuart to reject the offer. Stuart refused. Richard knew that Mavis would never sell the museum, so he decided to remove Stuart from the equation."

"Richard set about creating a sizable weapon. Not quite a sword, not quite a spear, but large and very deadly. I'm guessing he didn't have much knowledge of anatomy and he wanted to make sure that one good stab would kill Stuart instantly, no matter where it hit."

"Richard couldn't risk a struggle, as there would be several employees around. If Stuart had time to yell for help, his plan was sunk. Death had to be instantaneous," the inspector continued.

"After stabbing Stuart sometime between 9:00 and 9:45, Richard ran back to the forge and started melting down the weapon. He planned the murder a day before a blacksmithing class so, if anyone came in early, he could explain his presence and his activities."

"So far, I like this theory," said Jones thickly, through a mouthful of burger. "But will it hold up in court?"

"It'll be hard to prove for certain," replied the inspector. "DNA testing has improved immensely over the past decade, but you can't salvage much from something that has been melted down at 1600° C."

"So, what's the plan now?" asked Jones.

"With a weapon that size, things are bound to get a little messy," said Green cheerfully. "He had to carry the weapon back to the forge. I'll bet my boots that our team can find a few droplets of blood, now that we know exactly where to look. Let's ask the forensics team to go over the path to the forge, as well as the forge itself, with a fine-toothed comb."

***

The next day, with DNA tests in hand, they arrested Richard Fullom. He came with the detectives with the station without protest, eyes downcast. As she passed him off to another officer for booking, she couldn't help but feel a small surge of pride for a job well done.

"Well, Inspector, that's another case you've solved in less than 24 hours," said Jones with a smile as they walked back to their desks. "I guess you could say you're... ON FIRE!"

Case #6:
The Purloined Papers

Effington – October

Detective Bill Bronzeman climbed the stairs, sweat dripping from his brow. This was his last chance to catch the Unicorn Killer, the maniac who had been terrorizing Chicago for over two years. Bill had followed the trail to an abandoned warehouse in Washington Park. He heard a maniacal cackle echoing from the floors above. He clutched his gun and pushed the door open slowly with his foot…

Inspector Green's phone rang. Tearing herself away from the book she was reading, she looked at her mobile and groaned. It was Superintendent Young, and this wouldn't be a social call.

Superintendent Young apologized curtly for the late hour and got to business.

"Everything I'm about to say stays between us. Do you know Dr. Andrea Shearman? She also lives in Effington," asked the superintendent.

"I wave when I see her walking by and I'll chat with her at village events, but we're not close," replied Inspector Green. "Please tell me she hasn't murdered someone."

The superintendent replied, "No. You'll be surprised to learn that your friendly neighbor is one of the UK's top nuclear physicists. She's been conducting top-secret research for the past two years."

"Less than an hour ago, important papers summarizing a new finding disappeared from her house. Don't ask me for details about the contents of the papers, I don't have the security clearance," Young said gruffly.

"I've always been rubbish at physics," said Green. "I doubt I could make heads or tails of it, even if you gave me a copy of *Nuclear Physics for Dummies.*"

Young replied, "Always so self-deprecating, Green. But your solve rate speaks for itself. I'm trusting you to run this case alone for the next 12 hours. Come morning, we'll re-evaluate."

"Your job is to recover the missing papers as quickly and quietly as possible," he continued. "Dr. Shearman is expecting you. Call me when you have something, anything, to go on."

He rang off. Inspector Green looked at the book on the nightstand and sighed. The Unicorn Killer wouldn't be apprehended tonight, after all.

She got out of bed, changed out of her pajamas, ran a comb through her hair, and walked to the doctor's house.

***

Dr. Shearman ushered her into the living room. Andrea was a thin, energetic woman in her late thirties with long brown hair drawn up into a messy bun. She was wearing black yoga pants and a baggy blue T-shirt.

Although she usually had an easygoing demeanor and a smile on her face, tonight the doctor was in a state of complete panic. She immediately launched into an explanation.

"Thank you for coming, Inspector. Earlier tonight, I had three friends over for a dinner party," said Andrea, close to tears. "I bought a fondue set a few weeks ago —it was on sale for almost nothing, so I couldn't resist— and I wanted to try it out."

"Everyone arrived by 6:30 and we had a really lovely evening of wine and cheese," she went on quickly. "The fondue was smashing. Nothing seemed out of the ordinary."

Andrea continued, "I guess I should have locked my office door, but I've known each of these people for years! I trust them completely... or maybe I should say trusted? Sorry, I'm babbling, I'm still in shock. How could this have happened?!"

The inspector asked, "Let's take a step back. Is there any possibility that an outside intruder stole your papers?"

"No chance," Andrea replied. "I have motion-sensor lights and security cameras surrounding the house from every angle. I reviewed the footage after I called the police. There's not a sign of anyone entering or leaving the property other than my friends. It must have been someone in the house."

"Did any of your dinner guests leave the dining room for an extended period of time?" asked Inspector Green.

Andrea responded, "I knew you were going to ask me that. Each one left briefly, just once, to use the restroom. Also, around 8:00 p.m., I went down to the wine cellar to get another bottle of Merlot. Otherwise, no one left my sight all evening."

"What time did your guests head home?" the inspector followed up.

"I have an early flight to Washington D.C. tomorrow morning," said Andrea, rubbing her eyes. "Everyone left by 9:00 p.m. so I could finish some last-minute packing. I was just about to head upstairs when I noticed that my office door was slightly ajar."

She continued, "I went over to take a look, even though I thought I was just being paranoid. And I'm so glad I checked! I'll be in D.C. for two full weeks, so I wouldn't have discovered the theft until after I got back."

"When I saw that the safe was open, I called the police immediately. I didn't touch a thing," Andrea concluded. "I hope that was the right thing to do in this situation."

"You've been very helpful thus far. Can I take a look at your office?" said the inspector.

The doctor led her into a large, minimally decorated home office. On the left side of the room was a chalkboard covered in calculations. Inspector Green scanned it and wished that she had paid more attention in physics class. Anything beyond $E = mc^2$ was completely out of her grasp.

The office's back wall was dominated by an enormous metal desk. The inspector's eye was immediately drawn to the sizable fish tank sitting on the left side of the desk.

Although it was a large tank brimming with water, crammed full of plants and pirate-themed decorations, there were just three small goldfish drifting gently around inside.

One fish swam up towards the front of the tank and locked eyes with the inspector, then drifted gently back to the bottom to nibble on some gravel. Not the ideal witness, the inspector thought to herself.

Next to the fish tank, there was a small stack of paper. The inspector noted that there were a few drops of water on the corner of the top page. Otherwise, the metal surface of the desk was dry.

There was also a photo of an austere-looking woman that Inspector Green didn't recognize and a collection of elaborate fountain pens. It seemed that the doctor favored working with chalk, paper, and pen instead of modern electronics. Unusual, but not necessarily suspicious.

The inspector then turned her attention to the large metal wall safe on the right wall. Its door hung open and it was completely empty. The inspector swung the door shut and noticed that it did not have a combination lock as she expected, but a lock requiring a key. She turned to Andrea, who had been anxiously watching the proceedings.

"Where do you keep the key for the safe?" asked the inspector.

"Isaac, Niels, and Albert guard it," Andrea said, smiling a little as she pointed at the fishbowl. "Do you see that little treasure chest at the bottom of their tank? I keep it in there. You just take off the top of the tank, reach in your arm, and flip open the lid of the chest."

The inspector asked, "Did any of your friends know about your hiding place?"

"I may have alluded to the fact once or twice," Andrea admitted guiltily. "I liked the idea of having 'attack goldfish' guarding the key. Never in my wildest dreams did I think any of them would ever steal from me. I mean, none of them are even scientists!"

Andrea leaned against the wall, clearly exhausted by the stress and the late hour.

She continued, "The only reason they would possibly take my research is to sell it on the black market. I guess it could be worth a lot of money to the right person."

As she was talking, the inspector returned to the fish tank to give it a closer look. She crouched down and swept her fingers along the floor around the desk, feeling nothing but the softness of the gray carpet. She stood up, Dr. Shearman watching her curiously.

Inspector Green gave the office one last glance as they walked back into the living room. "I won't take up too much more of your time," the inspector said. "Can you give me a brief description of each of your party guests? Just the basics."

"Of course," responded Andrea. She took a deep breath.

***

"I've known Oscar Critchfield since we were about six years old. We met at infant school and have stayed close ever since. He works as the butcher in town. He's over six feet tall, with bright red hair and a matching beard. You may have noticed him clomping around town in his big black combat boots."

"Oscar got into powerlifting a few years ago and now competes in regional tournaments. He's very dedicated and spends an hour per day lifting weights. His biceps are the size of my head. He looks quite intimidating, but he's actually very soft-spoken. He loves jigsaw puzzles and his pet budgerigar, Bernie."

"Oscar didn't act unusual tonight, but he did tell us that his business is having financial trouble recently. More and more people are going to the Tesco in Hazelford instead of his shop, and he's a bit worried about money. I told him I could give him a loan if he ever finds himself in hot water, but he refused."

"I simply can't imagine Oscar would betray me like this. He's always been an extremely loyal friend."

***

"Christoph Bechert also attended tonight's party. I've known him since he moved here from Munich 10 years ago. He has the most delightful German accent and he's an amazing story-teller. Such a great sense of humor."

"Christoph works at Johnson's Bakery and—he wouldn't mind me saying this—it definitely shows! He enjoys sampling the merchandise, so he's got to be over 25 stone at this point."

"Despite the extra weight, he's actually a very graceful man. He's very involved in the local ballroom dancing community. He's been trying to convince me to learn to waltz for years, but I'm not interested. I don't want to hold hands with a stranger while they step on my feet."

"What else… Christoph has long, delicate fingers and can play the piano beautifully. He actually played a few songs for us tonight that he composed himself. I was very impressed!"

"Christoph has a heart of gold. I really don't think he would do anything like this."

***

"My last guest tonight was Rose Durrance. If I had to describe Rose in one word, it would be artistic. She owns an art studio across town and she's very talented."

"Rose does a little bit of everything: ceramics, painting, sculpture, you name it. She's probably most well-known for her elaborately carved wooden candlesticks. They're stunning! I have a pair on my dining room table right now."

"We met in our first year of university—I was studying physics; she was studying art history— and we hit it off immediately. She's a very empathetic person and an amazing listener."

"You've probably seen Rose around town, actually. She has short blond hair with the tips dyed pink. She's tall and slender. She looks like a catwalk model, but she's always wearing paint-splattered overalls. You can't miss her."

"I trust Rose completely. She knows how important my research is to me, and she's very supportive."

***

Dr. Shearman finished her descriptions and looked at the detective expectantly. "Was any of that helpful?"

"Yes, thank you. Obviously, I'll need to speak with each of these individuals as soon as possible," said Inspector Green. "But from what you've said and what I've seen, there's one person who's at the top of my list."

Who does Inspector Green suspect: the butcher, the baker, or the candlestick maker?

HINTS

HINT #1:
The thief reached in and took the key from the fish tank. They didn't use any special tools.

HINT #2:
The large metal desk was completely dry, other than a drop or two.

HINT #3:
Dr. Shearman and Rose have similar sized arms.

ANSWER

Inspector Green drove across Effington to a small brick house with ivy growing up the wall. She knocked sharply on the front door and waited.

Rose Durrance answered the door after a few moments. She was a very beautiful woman, just as Andrea had described. She had a small smudge of blue paint on her cheek.

"Can I help you?" she asked.

"My name is Inspector Green. I'm with the Dartshire Police Department. I'm sorry for the late hour, but I need to ask you a few questions. It's an urgent matter," said the inspector.

"Of course, come right in," replied Rose. She didn't seem too surprised by the intrusion. She ushered the inspector into a small living room.

The walls were covered in bright modern artwork. Two cats lay on the blue velvet sofa, ignoring the inspector. She decided to remain standing to avoid getting covered in white fur.

"How can I be of service?" Rose said politely.

"I'm sorry to say that there has been a theft at Dr. Shearman's home," said Inspector Green. "Can you tell us about your movements once you left the dinner party?"

"Something has been stolen? That's terrible!" responded Rose. "I left her house a few minutes before 9:00 and came straight home. I've been here since, working on an oil painting. I'm a night owl, so I usually don't go to sleep until 2:00 a.m. or so."

Inspector Green looked at Rose thoughtfully before asking, "Unfortunately, the culprit must have been someone attending the dinner party. You know all of those people quite well, including Dr. Shearman. Who do you think I should focus on?"

Rose replied, "Well, if I had to pick someone… it sounds like Oscar is having serious financial trouble. I wouldn't be too surprised if it turns out he's the one who took her papers."

"Well, now you've piqued my interest," said the inspector. "I hadn't yet mentioned what had been stolen. The doctor owns a number of expensive electronics, so why did you assume the papers were missing?"

Rose's composure faltered. "I… I…"

"Let's take a look at this painting you're working on, shall we?" Before Rose could object, the inspector moved quickly into the other room, where a large oil painting of a ship stood on an easel. One of the cats followed her.

Inspector Green surveyed the painting closely and noticed a slight rectangular bulge near the ship's hull. She scraped the freshly applied paint off with her hand, revealing a large envelope.

She turned around to face Rose, who stood watching the inspector, mouth agape.

"It wasn't a bad plan, Rose," said the inspector casually. "Take the papers, tape them to a canvas, cover them in thick layers of oil paint, and then sell the painting to the highest bidder."

"No one would have questioned you selling your artwork. You didn't expect the theft to be discovered for weeks, and by then, the papers would have been long gone," said Green.

"But how could you have possibly known that I was the one who took them?" asked Rose in disbelief. She looked utterly defeated.

"The fish tank in Dr. Shearman's office was brimming with water," responded the inspector. "If someone with a large arm had reached inside to get the key from the treasure chest, it would have displaced enough water to spill out onto the desk."

"The papers on the desk and the surrounding floor were both dry, which means Oscar and Christoph could not have done it. I therefore suspected you, as well as the doctor herself, since you both have slender arms."

Rose's blue eyes slowly filled with tears. "I hated to do that to Andrea, but I really needed the money. I've been in debt for years, and I couldn't risk losing my house or my studio. I had to try something!"

"There are better ways of earning money than betraying your friends," said Green. "Now, you're going to have to come with me."

After reading Rose her rights and taking her to the police station, the inspector finally made it back home around 2:30 in the morning.

She walked into her bedroom and looked forlornly at the book waiting on the bedside table. She could wait until tomorrow to find out who the Unicorn Killer was. She'd had enough excitement for one evening!

Case #7:
The Murdered Recluse

Petersborne – November

Edgar Tilbury was a loner. For the past 20 years, he had lived in the same tiny cottage on the edge of Petersborne without running water, electricity, or internet service.

He grew all his own food on the 12 acres of land surrounding his shack and sometimes foraged for mushrooms deep in the woods. Edgar occasionally came into town to buy essentials, but when he did, he rarely spoke more than a few words to anyone.

A quiet old man living a solitary life just outside a small, charming English village. No criminal record whatsoever. The kind of person that the entire town agreed was a bit of an odd duck, but ultimately harmless.

Edgar's body was discovered on the night of Halloween by a group of local teenagers who dared each other to touch the cottage's front door. They got more of a scare than they had bargained for when they looked through the cottage window and saw his rotting corpse, dead for weeks.

Everyone assumed it was a natural death, but the Dartshire County coroner decided to conduct an autopsy, just in case. He called Inspector Green immediately after receiving the results.

"The blood test showed high quantities of a synthetic poison called chlorofoxyl methalate in Tilbury's bloodstream," he said briskly. "It's specialist stuff. You're not going to find it in your village garden center. I'm sorry, but we've got a murder on our hands."

Inspector Green had a particularly tricky mystery to solve: who on earth had poisoned this old recluse, and how had they managed it?

***

Fortunately, despite his laconic nature, Edgar was a prolific writer who kept meticulous hand-written diaries detailing his daily activities. This included recipes, notes about wildlife activity, pressed leaves, and anything the old man deemed worth recording.

Constable Wilkes dropped the most recent journals at her desk, and the inspector flipped through them with interest.

"What do you think, Jones?" asked the inspector. "Shall we start at Tilbury's house? Or talk to the shopkeepers he saw on his last visit to town?"

Jones said, "I think we start with interviews. As far as we know, the shopkeepers were the last people to see Edgar alive. Maybe they can give us some insight into what the victim was like."

The drive to Petersborne took less time than usual, and the weather was cold but sunny. Green drove while Jones continued reading through Edgar's journals, occasionally reading interesting passages aloud.

"Annabel, did you know that you can use crickets to tell the temperature? Count the number of chirps in 25 seconds, divide by 3, then add 4," said Jones. "That will give you the temperature in Celsius."

"That's irrelevant to the case, but I'll keep it in mind the next time I go camping," replied Green. "Which, ideally, will be never."

Jones snorted and continued to leaf through the journals. They pulled onto the high street and parked in front of the stationery shop, Paper Palace. The shop's motto, painted on the window, was "We ROCK at paper and scissors!"

They entered the shop and asked for the manager, Clarice Nielsen. Clarice was a small woman of about 70, with bright blue eyes and white hair in a meticulously neat bun.

Edgar had purchased two reams of the shop's cheapest white paper, six spiral-bound notebooks, a set of charcoal sketching pencils, and 10 black ballpoint pens.

Clarice seemed nervous throughout the interview. From the minute the inspector introduced herself, Clarice kept adjusting her glasses and fidgeting with her hair. However, the inspector had interviewed hundreds of suspects who acted shiftily but turned out to be completely innocent. She would proceed without jumping to conclusions.

"You may be aware that we're treating Edgar Tilbury's death as a homicide, so I'll need to ask you a few questions," said Inspector Green. "We know that Edgar visited your store shortly before his death. Was his behavior out of the ordinary?"

"Not at all," replied Clarice. "I mean, he hardly said more than a sentence to me, but that's not unusual. That's just his way. He's turned into quite an odd man over the years."

"How long have you known Mr. Tilbury?" asked the inspector.

"Um, well, we've both lived in Petersborne all our lives," responded Clarice. "And... well, you'll find out sooner or later, so I might as well tell you. About 40 years ago, Edgar and I were romantically involved. We were actually engaged to be married when he left me for another woman." Color rose to her cheeks.

"I'm sorry to hear that," responded the inspector.

"Oh, that's all ancient history," said Clarice quickly. "Water under the bridge, as they say! I don't hold a grudge against him. I have this shop, my dog Mr. Biscuits, and a lovely life. It all turned out well in the end."

"Have you stayed in touch with him?" asked Jones.

"No," said Clarice. "We're polite when we see each other, but that's maybe a few times a year when he needs more pens and paper."

"Was there anyone who might want to hurt Mr. Tilbury?" asked Jones.

"Edgar didn't have any enemies. Or any friends. After his wife died, I think he was happy that way," said Clarice.

"Have you ever heard of a substance called chlorofoxyl methalate?" asked Jones, looking at Clarice closely.

She blinked several times. "No, that doesn't ring any bells. It sounds like a shampoo ingredient, maybe?"

"Thank you for your time, Clarice," said the inspector. "We'll be in touch if we have any additional questions. Here's my card if you remember anything that might come in handy."

***

Green and Jones walked across the street to the hardware store, C&T Supply. The store's owner was Edgar's only son, Noah Tilbury.

Noah was a tall man in his early thirties, with thick eyebrows and callused hands. At the hardware shop, Edgar had purchased gardening shears, several candles, and a large box of matches.

"I'm very sorry to hear about the loss of your father," said Inspector Green.

"Honestly, we weren't very close," replied Noah. "I'll miss him, of course, but it's not a devastating blow."

"You know Edgar better than anyone in the village," said the inspector. "Was he acting strangely the last time you saw him?"

"Not any more strangely than usual," said Noah, with a short laugh. "He asked for the items he needed and that was it. He didn't seem troubled, but Dad wouldn't have told me if he was having personal problems."

"As his sole heir, you'll be inheriting a sizable amount of money, as well as his land," said Inspector Green. "Were you aware that your father was well-off?"

Noah smiled broadly and responded, "I had no idea until his solicitor got in touch to share the news. He certainly didn't live like a rich man. It's a pleasant surprise."

"What do you plan to do with the money?" asked Sergeant Jones. "A few hundred thousand pounds probably changes things."

"I'm selling the land, and I'm selling this shop, and I'm getting out of here as soon as possible," said Noah. "I want to get a place in London and experience city life. I'm sick of being known as the hermit's son."

"Are you familiar with chlorofoxyl methalate?" asked Jones.

Noah's expression didn't change. "Never heard of it," he said. "Why?"

"It's relevant to the investigation," said Green. "That's all for now. We appreciate your assistance and we'll be in touch."

***

Last, Green and Jones walked down the block to Music N' More. The owner, Horace Montel, was a short, thin man in his mid-fifties with long, ink-stained fingers. Edgar had come in to have his banjo restrung, as it was no longer in tune.

Horace wasn't happy to have the police in his shop, but he agreed to a brief conversation.

"Mr. Tilbury was in your store for about 30 minutes while you fixed his banjo," said Inspector Green. "What did you two talk about?"

"You clearly never met Edgar," replied Horace in an annoyed voice. "He didn't do conversation. He spoke like every word was costing him money."

Horace continued, "Edgar stood at the front of the shop, looking out onto Bleeker Street the entire time he was here. I don't think we exchanged more than 10 words in total. You're wasting your time talking to me."

"You're probably not aware, but Edgar kept a detailed personal diary," said the inspector. "You're mentioned in there a few times. It seems you wanted to buy Edgar's land and you were... let's say… very persistent about it."

"What? I mean... what are you implying?" sputtered Horace. "Yes, I won't lie, I wanted that land. I wanted that land very badly. It's the perfect place for a new housing development."

"I broached the subject with Edgar every few months, but he was a stubborn old fellow," he continued. "No matter what price I offered him for his cottage, he wouldn't budge."

Horace became even more frantic. "But if you're saying I murdered him? Absolutely not! I won't say anything further without my solicitor."

He disappeared into the back office and shut the door firmly.

***

Sitting outside a coffee shop, Green and Jones reviewed their findings.

"If we're assuming that one of them did it, none of them had a very compelling motive," said Jones. "Revenge for a 40-year-old heartbreak? Expectation of a paltry inheritance? Desire for a specific plot of land? Murders have been committed for less, of course, but I'm not buying it."

"I agree," said Green, breaking off a piece of bagel. "Based on those conversations, I don't feel much closer to solving this case."

"That Horace was a real gem, huh?" replied Jones. "We didn't even get a chance to ask him about the poison before he threw us out."

"He wasn't what I would call cooperative," said Green. "Not that it matters. Normally I've developed a theory at this point, but I still haven't the foggiest idea what happened."

"Steady on, old girl," said Jones encouragingly. "We haven't even visited his cottage yet. Fancy walking there? It's a beautiful day."

"Sure, maybe some fresh air will stimulate our brains," said Green with a smile. She stood up and threw the remains of her bagel to a group of expectant pigeons. "Let's go check it out."

***

Twenty minutes later, the detectives stood in the entryway of Edgar's cottage and looked around. Based on what Inspector Green had heard about the old man, it wasn't quite what she had expected.

The bookshelves were the most eye-catching feature in the room. Two of the cottage's four walls consisted of floor-to-ceiling wooden shelves crammed with books. Inspector Green scanned the titles, many of which she recognized. About a quarter of the books were Edgar's older journals. She now understood why the man bought so many items from the stationery shop. He must go through several pages every single day.

Other than the books, the room was minimally furnished. There was a single bed in one corner and a small table with one chair. Inspector Green turned her attention to the battered leather armchair—the very chair where his body was discovered—and the large walnut side table covered in paper, pens, and melted-down candle stubs.

The inspector mentally gave thanks for electricity, especially in the frosty English winter, when the sun often sets before 4:00 in the afternoon. The small wooden stove in the corner couldn't have given off much heat. Even though the cabin was small, it must have gotten quite cold in the evenings.

Sergeant Jones spotted the recently-retuned banjo leaning against the wall in one corner. He picked it up and gave it a brief strumming. It sounded fine, but neither of the detectives knew anything about music. He also gave it a shake, just in case there was anything stored inside. No luck.

Green turned away from the armchair and noticed a wire birdcage on the floor near the stove. A small yellow canary lay dead on the floor of the cage.

"Oh, this is sad," said Green. "Look, Edgar had a little bird. I bet no one fed it after he passed. Or maybe it froze to death when there wasn't any heating. Poor thing."

"There's too much death in this town lately," said Jones, crouching next to the table and looking underneath. "But luckily we don't have to investigate that one." He removed the sheets and shook out the pillow on the bed.

Inspector Green sat down at the small table, mildly frustrated, and pulled out the coroner's report to read one more time. She read aloud, more for her own benefit than for the sergeant's.

"Edgar was in remarkably good shape for his age. The coroner didn't find a recent scratch or puncture wound on the body, so he wasn't injected with the poison. Chlorofoxyl methalate can't be absorbed through the skin, so it wasn't contact poisoning."

"Edgar grew all his own food. We've tested the fruits, vegetables, and soil outside the cottage and there was no trace of poison. The well where Edgar fetched his drinking water was also untouched. He did some foraging, but I doubt that someone would poison the forest's mushrooms and berries on the slight chance he would pick them."

"There were no signs of a break-in. The cottage's only door and all the windows were firmly locked when the kids arrived. No one besides Tilbury had a key to the cottage, and there's no sign that anyone else has even been inside this room."

The inspector sighed. Without a murder weapon or a plausible theory, this case was going nowhere. The general public may not care about the death of a strange, elderly man, but she hated to leave any case unsolved. Everyone deserved justice.

Inspector Green scanned the room again. If I just can figure out how the murder was committed, that will lead me to the culprit, she thought. Then she spotted it.

"Jones! That must have been how the murderer did it!" she half-shouted.

The sergeant jumped at the sudden exclamation. "Christ, Annabel, you nearly gave me a heart attack. Next time inspiration strikes, can you announce it a bit more quietly?"

"Oh, shush, you killjoy," said the inspector, putting on a pair of gloves. She picked something up and put it in the evidence bag. "If I'm right, this will prove everything!"

What did Inspector Green pick up from the cottage?

HINTS

HINT #1:
You should review the items that Edgar bought at each shop on his last visit to town.

HINT #2:
The cottage's lack of electricity is key, as Edgar often stayed up late while writing in his journal.

HINT #3:
Edgar and the bird both died the same way.

ANSWER

Inspector Green arrived at the lab in the late afternoon, out of breath. The laboratory technician, Jaidev Patel, looked up from his microscope quizzically.

"Can I help you, inspector?" he said.

"Yes, you can make my day by testing this candle immediately," said Inspector Green, between gasps for air. "And this dead canary, while you're at it."

"Wow, that's new," said Jaidev. "May I inquire as to what I'm looking for?"

"If my hunch is right, both should be full of poison," said the inspector. "It's called something like… chlorophyll marmalade? Don't laugh, the chemical name will be in the Tilbury file."

She went on, "Any chance you could squeeze it in before the end of the day? I'll buy you a pint at the Duck and Badger if you can manage it."

"You know I always prioritize your cases," replied Jaidev with a smile. "Let me finish testing these blood samples and then I'll get right to it. I'll call you with the results shortly."

Inspector Green returned to her desk and gave Jones a nod. She opened her inbox, groaned at the number of unread messages, and promptly closed it again. She started drumming her fingers on the wooden surface of her desk. The inspector had many virtues, but patience was not among them.

Constable Yardley walked by her desk. "Waiting on something?" he asked drily.

"Is it that obvious?" responded the inspector.

"Well, I can hear you tapping your fingers on your desk. You're also jiggling your leg. And you keep sighing loudly," said the constable. "You're not exactly the picture of tranquility."

"Give this man an award! Detective of the year!" said Inspector Green, throwing a ball of crumpled-up paper at his head.

Green continued, "I spent my day working on the Edgar Tilbury case. If the poison that killed him couldn't be absorbed by the skin, wasn't injected, and wasn't consumed, it stands to reason that it was inhaled. The canary was collateral damage. Now I'm just waiting on a call from–"

Her mobile phone started to ring. She grabbed it before the first ring ended.

"So? What did you find?" asked the inspector eagerly.

"You were right," said Jaidev. "I'll email you the analysis now. Is that enough for a conviction?"

"I think it's conclusive," said the inspector. "Whether Noah Tilbury knew about his inheritance or not, he intentionally sold his father a poisoned candle. I'm sure he assumed there would be no autopsy and the death would be attributed to natural causes."

"Let's go get that pint at the pub, and I'll pick him up in Petersborne first thing tomorrow," said Green.

She hung up and gestured to Jones and Yardley. "Drinks are on me if you two want to join. I'm feeling benevolent tonight!"

Jones smiled and gave the inspector a thumbs-up. "When it comes to generosity, Annabel, no one can hold a candle to you!"

Case #8:
Midnight Sacrifice

Pembley – December

Every muscle in Inspector Green's body tensed as she crept through the bushes towards the dark house. It was a quiet night, and the dense layer of snow on the ground seemed to absorb all sound.

The inspector scanned the area and saw the faint outlines of Sergeant Jones and several other colleagues silently moving into position around the house. They needed the element of surprise on their side.

The plan was simple: ram down the back door, flood the house with officers, locate the girl, and arrest the perpetrator. She glanced at her watch. The stakes couldn't be higher, and time was running out. The team had just under an hour to rescue her before it was too late.

The girl in question was 14-year-old Mary Applegate, kidnapped a week earlier while walking home from the local church. That would have been alarming in and of itself, but over the past few days, ominous flyers had started appearing all over the village.

"Citizens of Pembley, take heed! On December 12, as the clock strikes midnight, the second era of Jesus Christ will begin. One of the Lord's faithful followers will sacrifice the Virgin Mary on the sacred altar. Through this blood offering, a new world will spring forth. The corruption and wickedness of the past 2000 years will be wiped clean. All hail the Virgin Mary, savior of these evil souls. Her flowing blood will cleanse the impurities of the world!"

It was rambling nonsense, but the inspector knew that Mary's life was in grave danger.

In order to throw off the kidnapper's suspicions, Inspector Green had publicly announced that her chief suspect was an outsider passing through Pembley. However, the CCTV footage they had cobbled together from cameras around town showed no strangers in the neighborhood on the evening of the kidnapping.

That meant that one of four members of the Saint Theresa church committee likely committed the crime. It had been a bitterly cold night, and one of them must have offered the girl a ride home.

Crouching against the low brick wall, the inspector thought back to earlier that evening. At 9:00 p.m. there had been a church committee meeting. She had attended as a last resort, hoping that the culprit would give himself away.

--- TWO HOURS EARLIER --

The fresh snow crunched and squeaked underfoot as Inspector Green walked to the little village hall, tucked off to one side next to the vicarage. She imagined it had been the pride of Pembley once, but the Victorian brickwork gave a severe look to the building. A few lopsided strings of Christmas lights did little to cheer the mood.

Inside, she met the four members of the church committee: Mr. Ballard, Mr. Whitson, Mr. Sheffield, and Mr. Ames.

She had interviewed each one shortly after Mary's disappearance, but none of them had said or done anything that conclusively proved that they were involved in the kidnapping.

They sat around a large rectangular table, harshly lit by overhead fluorescent lights. Someone from the church had provided basic refreshments: bottled water, a tin of shortbread, some cheese biscuits, a fresh pot of coffee, and a bottle of wine.

Mr. Ballard, a tall man with a sharp jaw and short red hair, spoke first as he poured himself a large cup of coffee. "The weather really is unseasonably cold for mid-December," he declared. "I can't remember the last time we got this much snow." Weather was always a safe subject for conversation in England.

Mr. Whitson agreed heartily. He was a short, balding man whose speech was interrupted by the occasional stutter. "I was working to turn the compost heap in my back garden this afternoon, and my f-fingers were like icicles! Barbara bought me a pair of thick fleece gloves, but they barely made a d-difference."

Mr. Ballard responded, "It's exhausting work, especially in this weather, but it's well worth it! I'm sure your roses will show the benefits in the spring. Your flower garden is always the pride of the village."

Mr. Whitson said, with a note of pride in his voice, "Frozen fingers and sore muscles are a small price to pay for a g-gold medal in the Dartshire County Garden Show! I'm completely shattered, but it's nothing that an early night and some p-paracetamol won't cure."

Inspector Green noticed that Mr. Whitson's hands were shaking slightly as he brought the bottle of water to his lips. He then cleared his throat before continuing. "So, how about poor Mary then?"

Major Sheffield immediately chimed in. A retired army man, he had never said anything quietly in his life. "What a thing! What a horrible thing! In our village, of all places!" he barked. "Preposterous, I say!"

Sheffield was a big man, nearing retirement age but in great physical shape. During their interview last week, he had spent most of the conversation trying to convince Inspector Green to join the charity half-marathon he had organized.

The inspector had politely but firmly declined. She couldn't think of anything worse than getting up at the crack of dawn to run laps of the village in this freezing weather, but to each their own.

Sheffield continued loudly, "When I was over in Afghanistan, we had a translator kidnapped once. Poor fellow. Went by Hamish, or Habib, or something like that. I can't remember now. Long story short, they sent him back to the base, by post, over the next three weeks. Terrible show, it was…"

His voice trailed off as he realized that everyone was looking at him, horrified. He coughed and took a gulp of bottled water to hide his embarrassment.

Mr. Ames, his pale, pointed face glancing up for the first time, gave Major Sheffield a sour look. "Is that really a helpful thing to say at a time like this?" he asked sharply. "I mean, Mary was our responsibility. We brought her into the committee. If we hadn't, maybe this would never have happened…"

Mr. Ames' voice trailed off. He turned his attention back to his glass of white wine. The inspector had been quietly monitoring his intake. Less than five minutes into the meeting and he was already halfway through his second glass. Definitely a seasoned drinker, she thought to herself.

Breaking her resolve to stay silent throughout the meeting, Inspector Green asked, "Remind me, how did Mary become part of the church committee?"

Mr. Ballard answered, "We wanted to bring in some younger people. Mary joined our youth program and was keen to get more involved. She asked Mr. Ames here if she could join the church committee even though she was under 18. We all jumped at the idea."

Mr. Ames looked up with a jerk at the mention of his name. "Mary came to us knowing so little about the Lord," he said. "Her parents never took her to church when she was younger. I think they might be" –he lowered his voice to just above a whisper– "atheists!"

Major Sheffield barked, "Young ones aren't interested in the Lord these days! When I was a lad, every child in the village attended church. Every single one!"

"Those were the d-days," said Mr. Whitson.

Mr. Ames replied, slurring slightly, "Most teenagers just want to play video games and text each other nonsense. Mary was special."

A gloomy silence descended on the group. Ballard then said, "Mary IS special, not was. Anyway, we can't sit here speculating about Mary all night, we have work to do. Let's get down to church business."

The next 30 minutes involved much discussion of roofing repairs, the church's bell ringing policy (how late was too late?), and other parish trivialities. Mr. Whitson had to be nudged awake twice.

As the clock struck 10:00, Mr. Ballard drained the last dregs from the coffeepot.

He said briskly, "Well, gentlemen, I believe that concludes the business for this evening! Don't forget, next we'll need to finalize the set list for the Christmas Eve choir performance, so start brainstorming your favorite carols."

Major Sheffield stood up quickly. As he strode towards the door, he paused and said, "Inspector, are you sure there's no way you'll join us for the run tomorrow? It starts at 6:00 a.m., which I think is very reasonable. And it's for a good cause."

The inspector responded, "Thank you, major, but I'll leave the pre-dawn feats of endurance to you." The major laughed, grabbed his bicycle, and left the hall.

"The rest of us should get going as well," Whitson said. "It's c-cold out and the roads will only be getting icier. Ames, I know you usually walk home, but do you w-want a lift?"

Mr. Ames got unsteadily to his feet, having finished the entire bottle of wine during the course of the hour-long meeting.

"No thanks, old boy. The cold air is good for me!" He tottered out of the room, pulling his coat collar up high over his ears.

Mr. Whitson watched him go and shook his head slightly. He walked up to the inspector. "I hope you catch whoever took poor Mary," he said. "Don't hesitate to c-call me if you need any assistance." He stifled a yawn, apologized, and left the room.

Mr. Ballard ushered Inspector Green out of the hall and locked the wooden front door behind them. "I'm sorry if our little church meeting wasn't very exciting, inspector. Thank you again for coming. Have a nice evening!" He climbed into his red sedan and drove away.

The inspector watched the taillights fade into the darkness and thought back to the meeting. She now had a definite suspicion about one of the committee members.

It wasn't completely watertight, but with a case like this, it was enough to go on. She would call her team and start planning their attack.

The hoot of an owl snapped Green back to the present moment. She hoped that she had made the right call. The committee members had all seemed normal, but if 20 years of policework had taught her anything, it was that sometimes the craziest people can appear completely down-to-earth.

She glanced across the lawn at Sergeant Jones, who was awaiting her order. She gave him the hand signal to move. "Let's do this," she said to herself, under her breath.

Whose house is Inspector Green about to raid, and why?

HINTS

HINT #1:
It was the committee member's actions that alerted the inspector that something was awry, not the conversation at the meeting.

HINT #2:
One of the committee members seemed to be gearing up for a long night.

HINT #3:
Look at what each person was drinking at the meeting.

ANSWER

The officers broke open the flimsy back door with one kick. They streamed inside the house, checking each room for signs of the kidnapped girl or the perpetrator.

Inspector Green had only taken a few steps inside the house when she heard Sergeant Yardley yell from the basement, "Green! She's down here!"

The inspector descended the dark steps to the basement and found Mary Applegate tied to the radiator. Thank God, she was still alive! The girl looked equal parts terrified and relieved.

"Hello, Mary, we're with the Dartshire Police Department," said the inspector, cutting through her restraints. "We're getting you out of here. Do you know where he is?"

"I'm not sure," said Mary, rubbing her wrists. "He came down here earlier and said that things were almost ready. He seemed really excited. I heard him moving around upstairs but I don't know where he is."

Mary fixed her large brown eyes on the inspector as Sergeant Yardley took her arm and escorted her out of the room. "I don't think he's right in the head. Be careful!"

Once the inspector ensured that Mary was safely out of the house and in police custody, she joined her fellow officers in searching the building for the kidnapper.

They found a variety of concerning items: a red hooded ceremonial robe, six journals full of frenzied writing about the second era of Christ, dozens of photos of Mary taped to the refrigerator, and more.

Within a few minutes, there was only one place left to check: the roof. Inspector Green grabbed a flashlight, climbed the rickety stairs to the rooftop, and pushed open the metal door. She immediately saw the perpetrator standing on the other side of the flat roof.

"Hello, Mr. Ballard. Having a nice evening?"

Mr. Ballard turned and looked at the inspector with a manic glint in his eye. In the space of an hour, the respectable church committee member had disappeared. In front of her stood an unhinged man, capable of anything.

"You horrible woman, you've ruined everything!" hissed Mr. Ballard, balling his hands into fists. "Mary is the chosen one! And I am the Lord's faithful servant, ushering in a new age! Her blood must be spilled so that the world can be reborn!"

"Well, I don't mind this world," said the inspector with a shrug. "I think I'll sleep well at night knowing that I saved a young girl's life." She edged sideways out of the doorway, trying to keep the man's attention.

"You have no idea what you've done! You don't understand God's plan!" Ballard's voice rose to a shriek. "By stopping tonight's sacrifice, you have doomed our world to thousands more years of depravity and chaos!"

The inspector decided to try a different tack. "Ballard, we can get you the help you need," she said soothingly. "Just come with me downstairs and we can discuss your options."

"I don't want OPTIONS. If I can't live in the second era of Christ, I don't want to live at all!" Ballard moved towards the edge of the snow-covered rooftop.

Luckily, Inspector Green had distracted Ballard long enough for Sergeant Yardley to pass through the door unnoticed and sidle up behind him. As soon as Ballard started walking, the sergeant deftly tackled the man. The inspector moved quickly, pulling Ballard's hands behind his back and handcuffing him.

"No overdramatic suicides on my watch," said the inspector to herself as Yardley led Ballard away. "Mainly because it would generate far too much paperwork."

She made her way back downstairs into the main house, where she spotted Sergeant Jones bagging up evidence.

He gave her a thumbs-up and said, "It's been a hectic evening, and I didn't get a chance to ask before we charged in. What made you suspect Ballard over the other three?"

She replied, "It was really a process of elimination. Ames had drunk himself into a wine-induced stupor over the course of the meeting. I suspect he passed out within a few minutes of getting home. He certainly wasn't in any state to stay up several more hours and commit murder. He also never drove home from meetings, so how would he have picked Mary up?"

The inspector continued, "Sheffield was in the habit of biking to meetings regardless of the weather. Also, he organized a half-marathon for tomorrow morning. He'll be up around 5:00 a.m. setting out the course. I don't know about you, but I wouldn't plan a midnight sacrifice knowing I had to be up at the crack of dawn."

"Whitson spent the majority of today doing strenuous lawn work, so he was physically exhausted," said Inspector Green. "He almost nodded off several times during the meeting. Combine that with the fact that he's married: I couldn't see how he could keep Mary prisoner in his house for a week without raising his wife's suspicions."

"Now, Ballard sounded normal during the meeting," said Green. "But the man finished an entire pot of coffee by himself at 9:00 in the evening. A cup of coffee, I wouldn't have raised an eyebrow. But a pot? He had late-night plans that he needed to be awake for. Therefore, he was the most likely culprit."

"An impressive leap of logic," said Jones. "Let's bag up this evidence and go get some sleep ourselves."

Case #9:
The Escape Room

Norchester – January

Two young couples, bundled up in puffy jackets and woolly hats, walked arm-in-arm down Bradford Street. Their laughter echoed down the narrow alley before it was swallowed by the cold, dense fog.

"I'm still not sure if this is a good idea," said Gemma. "I don't much fancy being locked in a room for an hour. Especially with you lot!"

Louisa snorted and responded, "You're going to have fun, Gem, I promise. I did an escape room in Brighton last summer and had a blast. It's just a bunch of different puzzles to solve. It's not scary."

Adam added, "I don't even think they're allowed to actually lock you up. It's against fire regulations or something. So, if you can't stand one more minute in a room with us, you're free to scarper."

"Plus, we're all brilliant!" Louisa said cheerfully. "I'm sure we'll be out of there in 30 minutes or less, then we can go get dinner. Is it bad that I'm already hungry?"

"Lou, you're a bottomless pit," said Adam. "But I love you anyway. Oh, we're here!"

The group came to a stop in front of a nondescript brick building with a large white key painted on the front door.

"What's the theme of the room again?" asked Adam, holding the door open for everyone as they walked inside.

"Ancient Egypt," said Jacob. "According to the website, we're a group of explorers who have to escape from the pharaoh's tomb. If we don't make it out in an hour, we'll be cursed forever."

"I love that," laughed Louisa. "Bring on the mummies!"

"It's supposed to be their hardest escape room," continued Jacob. "The room is almost completely dark at first. I think there's one flickering torch on the wall."

"Oh, I don't like that one bit. If a mummy touches me in the dark, I will literally have a heart attack," said Gemma, feigning terror.

"It's not a haunted house, you silly goose," laughed Jacob, putting an arm around Gemma's waist. "There aren't actors waiting to pop out and scare you."

"Well, if a mummy gets me, I've left all my earthly belongings to you, babe," said Gemma. "Except my clothes. Louisa called dibs on those when we were about twelve."

"That's fair," said Jacob. "I don't think I would look very good in a crop top anyways."

As Gemma playfully swatted Jacob, a bearded man walked into the lobby and greeted them.

"Welcome to The Great Escape Rooms," he said. "You've booked under the name Jacob Bentmer, correct? I'm Cameron. I'll be your guide for tonight's Egypt Adventure."

"One quick thing before I get started," Cameron continued. "We were supposed to have a small group completing our Spy Adventure room tonight."

He went on, "However, several of those people had to cancel last-minute and only one person arrived. His name is Nathan. Would you mind if he joined your group? We'll give you a £10 discount."

He gestured to his left at a short, pale young man sitting in the corner. Nathan gave the group a crooked, hopeful smile.

"Sure, that's fine," said Jacob, ignoring Gemma's pointed stare. He knew she wasn't very keen on strangers, but he wasn't going to turn down a tenner. "He can join our team."

"Great!" said Cameron. "It will be easier for you to complete all of the puzzles with five people. It's our most difficult room by far. Only 20% of teams escape the tomb before time runs out."

"We're ready for a challenge!" said Jacob confidently.

Adam looked over at Louisa and was surprised to see a tense, almost angry look on her face. She was usually very easy-going, so he made a mental note to check on her after they got inside the room.

Cameron continued, "Let's get started! Please hand over all of your belongings, including wallets and phones, before the game begins. I'll keep an eye on them while you're inside."

He gathered everything in a cardboard box, then led them down a long hallway. They passed "Jailbreak Adventure" and "Pirate Adventure" before arriving at a door labeled "Egypt Adventure." Cameron pushed the door open and the group walked inside.

***

The room was large and quite dark. Looking around, the group could see painted hieroglyphs covering the walls. The room was dotted with several alcoves holding jars, most with heads of Egyptian gods. There was a large sarcophagus against the wall on the left.

"I knew it would be dark, but is it supposed to be this dark?" asked Gemma nervously.

"Yes, but don't worry. The solution to the first puzzle will prove quite illuminating," said Cameron with a smile.

He continued, "I'll be watching your progress over the video monitor, and you can use this radio to ask me for clues if you get stuck. You're limited to five clues per game, so use them wisely. Just press this button here."

"You'll have one full hour to complete all of the puzzles. The remaining time is displayed on that timer just above the door. Your time starts now. Good luck!"

He closed the door and the red timer on the wall started counting down from 60:00. Egyptian music started playing softly from a speaker in the corner.

"Well, let's divide and conquer," said Jacob. "Look for numbers, letters, locks, and keys. Like these! See, these pyramids scattered around the floor have Roman numerals on their faces. I bet they form a code."

The room descended into a flurry of activity. Adam found the notebook of Cyril Aldred, an explorer who had perished in the tomb years before. He tried to read it in the dim light and wished he had his phone.

Jacob attempted to open the sarcophagus but it was locked tight, so he moved on to the canopic jars that held the mummy's organs. He found a silver cat figurine hidden inside one of the lids. Shaking it, he could hear something rattling inside.

Louisa opened a chest and found about 20 tattered pieces of cloth. She started to fit them together and, squinting, realized she was building a map of Cairo. She felt a slight sting on the side of her neck but ignored it.

Gemma, overcoming her initial hesitance, picked up a laser pointer and started aiming it at various hieroglyphs on the wall to see if the light would open anything.

Nathan discovered the outline of a hidden door built into the wall and was trying to figure out what mechanism controlled it. He also found a oddly-shaped black key buried in a small pile of sand in the corner.

As she continued assembling the map, Louisa started to feel a bit light-headed. Not wanting to make a scene, she leaned against a wall and took a few deep breaths.

The other group members were engrossed in finding clues around the room, so no one noticed that Louisa had stopped working. She started to lose consciousness and slowly slid to the floor.

Adam said as he turned, "Hey Lou, I think we have to connect–"

He stopped as he spotted her on the floor. "Lou?" He walked closer and knelt down. He couldn't see her face well in the dim light.

"Honey, are you okay?" As he gently touched her shoulder, her head lolled to the side. He realized that something unthinkable had happened. Louisa was dead!

***

Less than an hour later, Inspector Green and Sergeant Jones walked into the Egypt Adventure room.

The young woman still sat slumped over in the corner underneath a painting of the goddess Isis. There were several marble-sized pyramids scattered around the body.

With the lights fully on, the room was significantly less impressive. It was clear most of the statues were made of papier-mâché, and not by an expert hand. The painted hieroglyphs were cracked and peeling in places. This was a room that was designed to be seen by flickering lamps, not harsh fluorescent lighting.

"The good news: we have an exact time of death and there were just four other people in the room when it happened," said Sergeant Jones.

"The bad news: nobody saw anything. They needed to build a statue of Osiris to turn the lights on, but they hadn't made it that far. They had been in the room about four minutes when Ms. Crowley died."

"Have we determined cause of death?" asked Green, scanning the room.

"Well, Dr. Kingsley noticed a pinprick on her neck and took a blood sample to the lab for analysis," said Jones. "It might be natural causes, but my bet is that she was injected with something lethal. Whatever it was, it must have been extremely fast-acting."

"Let's continue to treat this as a homicide until proven otherwise," said Green. "I assume the video feed from the room to the main desk isn't recorded?"

"No. The people who work as guides here can see and hear what the participants are up to, but the footage isn't saved anywhere," said Jones. "There's not really a point in keeping it."

"I've spoken briefly to the group, but now that you've arrived, shall we speak to each of them one by one?" asked Jones. "Constable Yardley is keeping an eye on them in the lobby."

He continued, "I've turned the Jailbreak Adventure room into a makeshift interview space. Maybe being in jail will test our culprit's nerves."

"Oh, that's a nice touch," said the inspector. "I like your style. Let's take a quick look at the victim's mobile phone before we start interviewing witnesses. With any luck, we'll catch someone in a lie."

Jones fetched Louisa's purse. As he pulled out a mobile phone, Inspector Green noticed a blood sugar monitor in the bag. Louisa must have been diabetic.

The inspector took the phone and scrolled through the incoming/outgoing calls. "Not much here, I'm afraid," she said.

"Green, do you know nothing about millennials?" said Jones with a smile. "People under age 40 hate talking on the phone. Check the text messages."

She snorted and handed the phone to him. "Be my guest. Work your youthful magic."

He started scrolling quickly through the messages. "Okay... there are a number of texts between Louisa and Adam. All seem normal for a newly engaged couple. Lots of hearts and kisses."

"Oh, the text chain with Jacob is more interesting... it seems like there's a one-sided flirtation. She tactfully rejects him at every turn. That can't have made his wife happy."

Jones continued, "And speaking of Gemma, there's no text history at all. A bit odd, that."

"We'll see what each of them has to say for themselves. I'd like to start the interviews with the victim's fiancé," said the inspector.

***

They walked two doors down. Mercifully, 'Jailbreak Adventure' included a large table and several chairs. They were soon joined by Adam Conway, who looked pale and confused. He was a slender blond man with thick-rimmed glasses and a plaid shirt.

He sat down across from the detectives and waited for them to speak.

"Adam, thank you for joining us. We know you've had a great shock," said Inspector Green. "Can you tell us, in your own words, what happened this evening?"

"That's the thing, I don't know what happened," said Adam. "One minute, we were all working on clues and codes in the dark. The next minute, Louisa is on the ground, dead. It happened so fast. Was it an aneurysm?"

"We have yet to determine the cause of death, but we'll let you know," said Green. "How long have you and Louisa been together?"

"About three years," said Adam. "I proposed two months ago on a trip to Paris, and we're—we were—scheduled to get married next fall. I can't believe she's gone."

"You would say your relationship was good?" asked Jones.

"Well, I don't go around proposing to people I don't like, now do I?" said Adam. He paused briefly. "I'm sorry, that was rude. Louisa and I were completely in love. Our relationship was as good as it gets."

"I do want to mention one thing," said Adam. "When we were in the lobby, I looked over at Lou and noticed that she looked tense, maybe even upset. I feel like maybe she knew that Nathan bloke? Or maybe she already wasn't feeling well? I meant to ask her about it but I never got the chance."

"Thank you, Adam," said the inspector. "You can return to the lobby. Please ask Jacob Bentmer to come join us."

***

As they waited, Jones' mobile buzzed. He looked down and saw a text from Jaidev Patel, the laboratory technician. The text read, "Blood test positive for poison. Will email you the full report now." He showed it to Green, who nodded as Jacob walked in and sat down.

Jacob was a short, muscular man with red hair. He crossed his powerful, freckled arms across his chest and sat back in his chair.

"Hello, Jacob," said the inspector. "You made the booking for the room, correct?"

"Yeah," said Jacob morosely. "It was a belated birthday present for Louisa. It was Gemma's idea, actually. My wife."

"How long have you known Louisa?" asked the inspector.

"Gemma and Louisa met after university," said Jacob. "They both worked at the same advertising agency. I started dating Gemma and was eventually introduced to Louisa at a party about four years ago."

"Did you know her well?" asked Jones.

Jacob shifted uncomfortably in his seat. "Not very well, no. She's more Gemma's friend than mine. They talk about girl stuff."

"Can you explain why you've sent her hundreds of texts in the past month, then?" asked Jones. "I would say messages like 'Adam is a lucky man ;-)' suggest a relatively close relationship."

Jacob looked briefly shocked, but recovered quickly. "Hey, I'm a flirt, what can I say?" he said. "That's just how I communicate."

"So, Gemma knows all about these messages you've been sending?" asked Jones.

"She doesn't mind," said Jacob. "She's not insecure. She knows our marriage is solid."

"Great, we'll be sure to ask her about that," said Jones. "Let's get back to what happened tonight. What did you see after you entered the escape room?"

"We all walked in, the guy who works here gave us the spiel about timing, then he closed the door and left," said Jacob. "It was so dark in there. You couldn't see a thing. We all spread out and started working on different tasks."

"After a few minutes, Adam noticed that Louisa was on the floor and shouted for help. The escape room guy opened the door and called an ambulance. She was dead before he even made the call, though."

"What do you think happened?" asked Inspector Green.

"I don't know, some sort of blood clot or something? I don't know what could kill someone our age that fast," said Jacob. "She seemed completely healthy."

"Thank you for your time. We'll let you know if we have any additional questions. Please send in Gemma," said the inspector.

***

Gemma Bentmer entered the room. Petite, dark-haired, with pointy elfin ears, she was barely holding it together.

"I c-can't believe it," she stammered. "I can't believe she's gone. Was it diabetic shock? No one has told us what happened yet."

"I'm sorry, we can't share the cause of death at this time," said the inspector. "Did you see or hear anything suspicious after you had entered the escape room?"

"Well, it was pitch black in there," said Gemma. "And that Egyptian music was playing the whole time. It was a bit distracting."

She continued, "But I will say that at one point I heard a whirring noise, like something mechanical. I assumed someone had solved a puzzle or something."

"Did you know that your husband was sending flirtatious texts to Louisa?" asked Sergeant Jones.

Gemma's thin lips compressed into an even thinner line. "Yes, Louisa told me about them. She didn't think it was appropriate. I haven't talked to Jacob about it yet, but I was planning to this weekend."

"Louisa definitely has a knack for getting people to fall in love with her," continued Gemma. "When we worked together at Fosters Advertising, about half the men there asked her out. She can't help it. She's just so beautiful."

"Have you and Louisa texted each other at all in the past few weeks?" asked Inspector Green.

"Yeah, we text a fair amount," said Gemma. "You can check my phone and see all of our conversations. It's not very interesting, I'm afraid. We're planning a trip to Switzerland next spring and…"

Gemma realized that she should be talking about her friend in the past tense and started hyperventilating. "I'm sorry–I just need a minute–"

"That's fine, Gemma," said Inspector Green. "You can go back to the lobby for now. Maybe go to the bathroom first and splash some water on your face. I always find that helps me calm down. Will you ask Nathan to come in?"

***

Nathan Forrester entered the room and stood across from the detectives. "I'd prefer to stand, if that's all right," he said.

"That's fine," said Inspector Green. "I've been told that you weren't acquainted with any of the other people in the group. How did you end up in their escape room?"

"Well, I was supposed to be doing the Spy Room with two friends of mine, a couple," Nathan said, sullenly. "But they called me only 10 minutes before our scheduled start time and said they couldn't come."

"Their dog Buster was sick and they didn't want to leave him. I was already here, so I asked the guy at the main desk if I could join another group. I guess that was a mistake."

"Did you know Louisa Crowley? Had you ever seen her before?" asked the inspector.

"I've never laid eyes on any of those people in my life," said Nathan emphatically. "I was just excited to try a new escape room. I've done over 20 different ones around England at this point. But after tonight, I don't know if I'll ever go back."

"Did you see or hear anything unusual while you were in the room?" asked Green.

"No, I was focused on trying to open a door hidden in the wall," said Nathan. "I wasn't paying attention to anyone else in the room. I wish I had been, though. I took a first-aid course last fall and maybe I could have helped provide CPR or something."

"Thank you, Nathan," said Inspector Green. "Please send in Cameron on your way out."

***

Cameron Murphy, a tall, thin man with a dark, close-cropped beard, sat down. "I can't believe this has happened," he said immediately. "I've been running these escape rooms for two years and we've never had a single issue."

"The business was doing well?" asked Sergeant Jones.

"Yes, my uncle died a few years ago and left me a small inheritance," said Cameron. "I left my job working at a local grocery store and started this place. Business has been steadily growing. We have great reviews online."

"Do you usually act as a guide?" asked the inspector.

"No, I mostly just run the business," said Cameron. "Marketing, finances, and all that. Normally I don't supervise the rooms, but we're short-staffed tonight."

"Did you know any of the participants?" asked Inspector Green.

"As a matter of fact, I did," said Cameron. "I went to secondary school and sixth-form college with Louisa. We didn't know each other very well, but I recognized her when she came in tonight."

The inspector asked, "You were watching the group over the monitor when it happened?"

"Yes, it was pretty dim though," said Cameron. "They hadn't yet assembled the statue of Osiris and put it in the wall. That activates the lights."

"Was anyone acting strange? Was there anyone who spent most of their time standing next to Louisa?" asked Jones.

"It's not the biggest room, and they were all within arm's length of Louisa at some point," said Cameron with a shrug. "They were all moving around within the room, so any of them could have injected her."

"Did you design each room yourself?" asked Inspector Green.

"Yes," said Cameron with a hint of pride in his voice. "I don't have an engineering degree or anything, but I've always been good at making mechanical devices. I built all of the rooms here from scratch. I could give you an overview of the mechanisms in the Egypt room, if you would like?"

"Maybe another time, Mr. Murphy. Please return to the lobby and let everyone know it should only be a few more minutes before they're released," said Green.

Cameron nodded and left the room.

"We're letting everyone go?" said Sergeant Jones. "No offense, but that seems premature."

"Yet again, the murderer has slipped up," said Green. "If you think back through the interviews, you'll find that someone said too much."

Who does the inspector think poisoned Louisa Crowley, and why?

HINTS

HINT #1:
Someone was lying about their relationship with Louisa Crowley.

HINT #2:
Louisa Crowley saw someone she recognized, but it wasn't Nathan.

HINT #3:
Someone knew exactly how she was killed.

ANSWER

Jones scowled at her. "I hate it when you're secretive."

Green gave him a smirk and said, "All will be revealed in time, my friend. Will you ask Cameron Murphy to come back for one or two follow-up questions?"

Cameron re-entered the Jailbreak Adventure room. He looked expectantly at the inspector. "That was quick. What else can I help you with?"

"Well, a signed confession would make my life a lot easier," said Green.

Cameron looked at her blankly for a few moments. "I'm sorry, I don't know what you're talking about. I wasn't even in the room when it happened."

"That's right, you weren't," said Green. "Smart lad. How long did it take you to build the device that killed her?"

Cameron smiled weakly and looked over at Sergeant Jones. "Is she joking?"

"Not joking, I'm afraid," said Green sharply. "In our conversation just now, you were the only one knew that she was murdered. Everyone else assumed some sort of natural cause. That's a bit suspicious."

Cameron opened his mouth to protest but the inspector held up a hand.

"What's more, you knew how it was done. You said that anyone in the room could have injected Louisa with the poison," said Green. "We hadn't shared that she was poisoned, and even if we had, most people would have assumed it was something she ate or drank."

Cameron stared at the inspector, mouth agape.

"Now I'm venturing into speculation, but my guess is that you and Louisa have a history," said Green. "That's why she acted a bit upset before going into the escape room. She was surprised to see you."

Cameron slowly sat down on the chair, pale as a sheet. There was a full minute of silence. The inspector waited impatiently.

Cameron finally said, "I loved Louisa and she didn't love me. I've loved her for years, since we were kids. She never gave me a chance. It drove me insane."

"After sixth-form ended, she got a restraining order against me," he continued, with a slight scowl. "It expired a few months ago, so I texted her to see if she had changed her mind. She didn't respond."

"I've always held out hope that she would come around, but when she got engaged to Adam, I realized it was futile," said Cameron. "That's when I started thinking about killing her."

"At first, they were just idle fantasies. But then Jacob Bentmer booked a room for four people. I keep tabs on her, I know who she hangs out with. I asked Jacob to confirm the names of his party members, then I started to plan."

"You should have seen Louisa's face when she walked in and saw me behind the desk," he continued. "She wasn't happy, but she was never one to make a fuss."

"Once they were in the room, I took advantage of having her phone and deleted our text history," said Cameron. "I accidentally deleted her text chain with Gemma as well. Clicked the wrong button. Then I did the same on my phone. No one would know we communicated recently. No motive, a perfect alibi... I thought I had planned every detail."

"How exactly did you kill her?" asked Sergeant Jones.

"I built a spring-loaded contraption that I could trigger from the front desk," said Cameron. "It would spring out, deploy the poison on contact, and then retract back into the wall. The seams are damn near invisible under the paint."

"And, technically, I built six of them," he said, with a note of pride in his voice. "I didn't know where she would be standing and I needed to get her in the first few minutes of darkness."

"As soon as I had killed her, I knew I made a huge mistake. I regret it already. I will confess to everything, on the record. I'm ready to face the consequences," Cameron concluded.

Constable Yardley put Cameron in handcuffs and led him to a waiting police cruiser.

"A very satisfying conclusion to a puzzling case," said Jones. "Let's just hope he doesn't use his escape skills on whatever prison he ends up in."

Case #10:
The Blind Witness

Hazelford – February

Inspector Green had just returned from a luxurious two-week vacation in Madeira. She was uncharacteristically relaxed and had even acquired a slight tan, which Sergeant Yardley immediately commented upon.

"Is this truly our Annabel?" he quipped. "This tropical, bronzed goddess I see before me? Be still, my heart!"

Smiling, she responded, "Feast your eyes, Brian. I give it three days until I'm back to my normal lily-white self."

She sat down at her desk. She was ready for the usual lineup of petty crimes. Bring on the noise complaints and property line disputes! Even the thought of paperwork couldn't dull her post-vacation buzz.

Her mobile rang. It was Sergeant Jones.

"Hi, Jones," said Inspector Green. "I was wondering why you weren't in the office. Did you miss me while I was gone?"

"Desperately," replied Jones drily. "I don't know if the Dartford PD could have made it another week. But you have perfect timing. There was a murder yesterday."

The inspector sat up straight. "What? Where?"

"Hazelford. Meet me on Keller Street and I'll give you the details. It's gang-related," said Jones. "See you soon."

The inspector had started packing her bag before he had even finished his sentence, and she was on the way to Hazelford within minutes.

Hazelford was the least charming village in all of Dartshire, the county's one concession to modernity. Built in the 1960s, the town was 80% concrete with just one public park.

Hazelford was larger than the surrounding villages and offered a large supermarket and a shopping mall, but the inspector didn't spend much time there.

She arrived at Keller Street and managed to squeeze her car into a miniscule parking spot. Getting out of the sedan, she spotted Sergeant Jones across the street. He was smoking, as usual, and quickly threw away the butt of his cigarette when he saw her.

"Welcome back!" said Jones. "I thought we could walk to the scene of the crime. That way I can fill you in on what you missed while you were out of the office."

"Perfect, fire away," said Green.

"Are you familiar with the Merchants?" asked Jones.

"The name sounds familiar, but I can't place it," said Green. "Enlighten me."

"They're a criminal gang from east London who has been slowly expanding into more rural areas," said Jones. "Dartshire included."

"You know, I've been saying we needed some good, old-fashioned gang violence to liven things up," said Green. "What are they like?"

"Well, they're known for being utterly ruthless. They use a blend of violence, threats, and bribery to get what they want. Unfortunately for us, they're also very smart, according to my friends in the London PD."

"You should know the victim," continued Jones. "It was Kenny Shanklin."

Kenny Shanklin was a pickpocket, a burglar, a con artist, and an all-around opportunist who drifted from town to town around southern England. Inspector Green had busted him twice over the past few months.

Although he was certainly a fraud and a charlatan, she couldn't help feeling sorry for him. Regardless of his crooked ways, he was a likable rogue who didn't deserve to be killed.

"Poor bugger," said Green. "What happened?"

"We have a pretty good idea," said Jones. "One of the London cops, Inspector Prescott, gave me the rundown yesterday evening. They have an officer who's currently undercover with the Merchants, feeding them information."

"Kenny had agreed to act as a courier for the gang's Hazelford activities. He knew the roads, where the cops patrol, and so on. He was a good source of local knowledge."

He continued, "After less than a week on the job, the Merchants discovered that someone was skimming goods from each delivery. It didn't take them long to realize that their new courier was to blame."

Green nodded. This was a typical Kenny move. He had done it dozens of times before, but it wasn't something you should try with a gang like the Merchants.

"As a result, Shanklin was shot in in Harrows Park in broad daylight yesterday afternoon," said Jones, with a tinge of sadness in his voice. "Two .44 caliber bullets directly through the back of his skull."

"And they weren't exactly subtle about claiming responsibility," Jones went on. "They left a note on the body as a warning to anyone else who crossed the gang."

"But luck was on our side. Two local coppers happened to be passing the park at the exact moment the shots rang out. They ran over and were able to apprehend three gang members immediately," said the sergeant. "They've been in custody since."

"We don't know which one pulled the trigger, and that's what we need to find out," said Jones. "Without definitive proof, we won't be able to charge anyone for the crime."

They ducked under the police tape blocking the park's entrance and walked slowly around the perimeter.

"We recovered the gun, which was thrown in a flowerbed, and we've been able to isolate skin cells from the handle," Jones resumed after a short period of silence. "The lab is analyzing them now and we should have a full DNA profile shortly."

"Great, just test all three suspects and this case should be closed in no time," said Inspector Green as they passed by a rickety metal playground. "It's an open-and-shut case. I don't know why you even need me."

"Not so fast. The Merchants have been able to hire some incredible solicitors over the past few years," said the sergeant. "Their legal representatives convinced a judge earlier this year that testing their members *en masse* is police harassment and abuse of power."

"For this case, we're only allowed to test one of the suspects. If we pick the wrong one, they all go free," he said.

"That's absolutely ridiculous!" said Green.

"I know. It's absurd. But we have an ace up our sleeve," Jones responded. "We have a witness."

"Excellent! Can he or she identify the murderer?" said Green excitedly.

"Unfortunately, he didn't see anything," said Jones. "The man is completely blind. His name is Byron Fenton, a vagrant who was sleeping on a park bench at the time. We're hoping he might be able to identify the killer based on voice alone."

"Oh, here we are. This is where Shanklin's body was found."

Green looked down at the faint remains of dried blood on the cement walkway. Poor Kenny. She resolved to catch his killer, even if that meant provoking the anger of the Merchants.

"Do you see anything unusual?" asked the sergeant.

"No, I haven't noticed any footprints or evidence that the search team missed," replied Green. "They did a thorough job. But it's always useful to visit the scene of the crime."

"Let's head back to the station," said Jones. "We've set up a police lineup with the three suspects. Based on what the witness says, we can decide whose DNA to test."

***

Arriving back at the Dartshire Police Station, Green and Jones met the witness in a conference room. He was an older man with greying, unkempt hair and a ragged blue overcoat. They thanked him for coming in.

"Mr. Fenton, we're aware of your visual impairment," said Jones diplomatically. "However, you heard the culprit speak to the victim and run across the park, so you're our best shot at identifying the killer."

He continued, "We've gathered the three suspects and we've asked them to repeat the words you heard earlier. Are you ready?"

The man nodded nervously. "I know what happens to people who inform on gangs, though," he responded, with a surprisingly aristocratic accent. "Will they see me at any point? I don't want to be next on their list."

"No, all three suspects are being held in separate rooms. We'll bring them next door one at a time. We're behind mirrored glass, so they couldn't possibly identify you," Jones said soothingly.

Fenton breathed out. "All right, there's no time like the present. I'm ready."

***

Green buzzed the intercom and the first man trudged into the room. This was clearly not Carl Rabelo's first time in a police lineup.

He was a scar-faced brute of a man with a squashed nose and thick eyebrows. His voice was rough and rasping, ground down by decades of heavy smoking. He glared at his reflection in the mirrored glass.

Jones asked the man, "Please start by saying the line we've asked you to memorize."

Carl said gruffly, "You stupid wanker. You think you can steal from the Merchants? You will never steal again."

Sergeant Jones pressed the intercom button and said, "Great. Now, I know it's a small room but we're going to need you to run around the perimeter."

Carl sneered and said, "Real men don't run. The killer didn't run. I don't run."

"Nevertheless," replied Jones evenly, "Your solicitor promised that you would cooperate with us. You can run around that room right now or spend the night behind bars."

The big man grimaced and scowled before awkwardly jogging around the room with an unsteady stride. His large Doc Martens slapped the linoleum floor of the police station.

Carl completed two laps of the room before stopping and snarling, "Is that enough? I'm not training for the Olympics here."

"That will do," said Jones. "Thank you, Mr. Rabelo. You can return to the holding area."

***

The next suspect who walked into the room couldn't have been more different, in both looks and temperament. Harry Runyan had a black mustache and quick, darting eyes. He was short, skinny, and full of energy.

Jones pressed the intercom button and said, "Thank you for coming in, Mr. Runyan. Please start by saying the line."

Harry shifted from foot to foot while saying the line in a sharp nasal voice. "You stupid wanker! You think you can steal from the Merchants? You'll never steal again!"

He laughed nervously, a high-pitched titter that was more suited to a child than an adult man. "Did I get the phrasing right? My memory is no good! I can say it a few more times."

"Once is fine, Mr. Runyan," said Jones. "Now, can you please run a few laps around the interview room?"

Unlike Carl, Harry was more than willing to oblige. He was obviously a practiced runner, as he had an easy stride and chattered at the mirrored glass without getting out of breath.

"Any ideas then, who did it? Not me. Not me! But someone, for sure! Did you check the spelling on the note? How about the handwriting? You don't want to miss any clues!"

"Thank you for your valuable advice, Mr. Runyan," said Jones drily. "We'll keep that in mind moving forward. You can head back to the holding area now."

The third man entered the room. Frank Bramblitt was middle-aged, medium height, with hair that could have been described as either brown, blond, or red, depending on the light. He looked like an accountant, not a member of a violent criminal gang.

"How long is this going to take?" he asked. "I have lots of important business to attend to." His voice was unexpectedly smooth and mellow, the type of voice you would hear coming from a radio DJ on a jazz station.

"Just a few more minutes of your time, Mr. Bramblitt," said Sergeant Jones. "We just need you to say the line we asked you to memorize."

Frank sighed. "You stupid wanker, you think you can steal from the Merchants, but you will never steal again," he said.

"Now, please run around the room," said Jones. "Just a few laps will suffice."

"I have no idea what you're trying to achieve with this exercise, but let no one say I wasn't cooperative with the police," said Frank.

He took off running and Green noticed that he had a very unusual stride. He took high, springy steps and resembled a prancing horse.

"Thank you for indulging us, Mr. Bramblitt," said Jones. "We'll have an update on your release time shortly."

As Frank walked toward the door, he paused and looked directly at the mirrored glass. He said, "I wasn't there when it happened. I was by the swings, a long way from the murder. You have nothing, I repeat, NOTHING on me!"

With that unusual announcement, he swept out of the room. Despite Frank's nondescript appearance, Inspector Green could tell that the man was highly dangerous.

***

Inspector Green looked back at Fenton. He looked shaken and ill. "That must have been difficult for you. How about a cuppa?"

He nodded slightly and she fetched two cups of strong, hot tea. She waited impatiently as he took several sips of the steaming liquid.

As soon as color started coming back into his cheeks, she asked gently, "Now that you've heard all three suspects speak and run, what do you think?"

"I don't rightly know," he said weakly. "The voice of the murderer was so intense. It was harsh and mean, but I could hear every single word. It didn't sound like any of the three men we just heard… but maybe they were putting on a voice."

Fenton continued, "Also, the sound of the running footsteps didn't match with what I heard yesterday afternoon. The killer had an even stride but he sounded like a heavy man. I couldn't point to any of the three suspects and say it was him for sure."

Green and Jones exchanged an exasperated glance. This might have been a waste of time.

"If you had to bet on one of the three men, which would you pick?" asked Jones.

"If I *had* to pick? The first one, the ugly one," said Fenton. "He was closest to the voice but the sound of his running gait wasn't right. I can't swear on it in court."

"Mr. Fenton, you have been extremely helpful," said Inspector Green. "I'd like to discuss with my sergeant here and we will get back to you shortly. Would you like another cup of tea?"

Fenton shook his head. "I feel much better now, thank you."

"Well, feel free to have one of these ginger biscuits while we're gone," the inspector said, clearing away the mugs.

The detectives walked into the adjacent meeting room and sat down.

"I think it was the third suspect," said Jones, without preamble. "How did he know that the murder didn't take place by the swings?"

"I noticed that as well," said Green. "But unfortunately, each of our suspects said something incriminating today."

"The first suspect knew that the killer didn't run. The second suspect knew about the note on the body. The third knew where the murder took place. They're all in on it to some extent, and I think the goal is to prevent us from identifying the real perpetrator."

"I just wish that our witness had been able to pick one person conclusively," said Jones. "That would have made our life a lot easier. I suppose we'll have to charge all three as accessories to murder." He rested his chin on his hands.

Inspector Green said, "I can help you there. Someone did make a mistake. I think I know who to test."

Whose DNA is the inspector going to test?

HINTS

HINT #1:
Each of the three suspects knew exactly what had happened to Kenny.

HINT #2:
This case hinges on someone seeing something they weren't supposed to.

HINT #3:
The witness lied about something important.

ANSWER

Inspector Green said, "It was a clever plan, I'll admit. But the culprit went off-script and gave himself away. Typical. That's what you get for being overconfident."

Sergeant Jones gave her a withering look. "Just tell me which one to test. I'm not groveling this time."

The inspector said, "I'll cut to the chase. All three of the suspects we interviewed are accomplices to the crime, but Byron Fenton is the killer."

"Fenton?! The blind guy?" spluttered the sergeant in disbelief. "How would he even have known where to aim the gun?"

"Fenton has been lying to us from the start," said the inspector. "When you asked him who his prime suspect was, he said 'the ugly one'. If he was truly blind, he wouldn't have known anything about the suspect's looks."

"Oh my God, you're right," said Jones. "That remark totally slipped past me."

"I took away Fenton's tea mug," said Green, holding it up. "We can test the saliva on the cup and check if it matches the DNA profile from the gun."

She continued, "I suspect the point of this entire charade was to ensure that no matter which of the three suspects we tested, it wouldn't be a match."

"Let's go get that mug tested now and see if your theory is correct," said Jones. "There's no time to waste!"

***

An hour later, Green and Jones walked back into the room where they had left Byron Fenton to wait. Jones took the lead.

"We apologize for the delay, Mr. Fenton," he said cheerfully.

Fenton shrugged and said, "I don't mind sitting in here. It's much warmer here than it is outside. I can stay all afternoon."

"Well, I have two pieces of good news for you," said Jones.

"Oh, yeah?" said Fenton. "I'm glad to hear it."

"The first: with the help of your testimony, we've solved the case!" said Jones.

"Really?" said Fenton incredulously. He sat up in his seat. "Which of the three suspects did you arrest for the murder?"

"That actually takes me to my second piece of good news. You're going to be inside for a long time! British prisons have excellent heating systems," said Jones slyly.

"Wha... what?" said Fenton.

"Yes, sir, you are hereby under arrest. We took the DNA from your tea mug and compared it to the skin cells we found on the gun. What do you know, it was a perfect match!"

Jones went on, "We know you're not blind. We know your real name is Larry Baumeister. We know everything."

Fenton's face went from confused to shocked to enraged as Jones spoke. He stopped staring at the wall and locked eyes with the sergeant. He growled, "Oh, you'll regret this. You should never mess with the Merchants."

Unfazed, Jones replied, "Your gang will regret the day you ever came here. Kenny may have been a petty criminal, but he was also a local, a father, and a human being. In Dartshire, we look after our own."

"Now, these fine officers are going to take you to your holding cell," the sergeant concluded. "You might not be blind, but justice sure is."

YOU DID IT!!!

Wow, you made it through the entirety of the book. Congratulations! Weaker minds would have given up long ago.

Give yourself a pat on the back for completing 10 challenging mysteries. You are now a certified Smart Person.

If you enjoyed these stories and want more mental exercise, you can check the other titles in the *Books for Smart People* series.

Thanks for reading!

Did You Notice?

The character names in several of the whodunits are related to the story's theme.

Death at Dartford House – Adelson, Warner, and Ruffin are last names of hotel chain owners.

History Repeats Itself – Fullom, Beecroft, and Girdlestone are last names of 19th century British historical figures.

The Purloined Papers – Critchfield, Bechert, and Durrance are last names of notable physicists. Albert, Niels, and Isaac (the goldfish) are named after physicists as well.

The Blind Witness – Rabelo, Bramblitt, and Runyan are last names of notable artists/athletes with visual impairments.

Village Names

Dartshire is entirely fictional, as are all of the town names. I did a huge amount of cross-referencing village names, because many of the towns I originally created turned out to be actual places. Oops.

Here are just a few of the delightful real English village names that I came across while scanning through Google Maps:

- Chipping Norton
- Harrowbarrow
- Barton in the Beans
- Upton Snodsbury
- Newton Poppleford
- Doddycross
- Little Packington
- Crumplehorn
- Clapton-on-the-Hill
- Goonhavern
- Lower Eggleton
- Nab's Head
- Otterhampton
- Saltburn-by-the-Sea
- Wigglesworth

BOOKS FOR

SMART PEOPLE

<u>Titles include:</u>

Riddles for Smart People: Volume 1

Riddles for Smart People: Volume 2

Riddles for Smart Families: Volume 1

Whodunits for Smart People: Volume 1

<u>*Coming soon:*</u>

Games for Smart People: Volume 1

Printed in Great Britain
by Amazon